when you
*wish

ALSO AVAILABLE FROM
LAUREL-LEAF BOOKS

when you

you

wish

Kristin Harmel

LAUREL-LEAF BOOKS

Copyright © 2008 by Kristin Harmel

All rights reserved. Published by Laurel-Leaf,
an imprint of Random House Children's Books,
a division of Random House, Inc., New York.
Originally published in hardcover by Delacorte Press,
New York, in 2008.

Laurel-Leaf and the colophon are trademarks of Random House, Inc.

Visit us on the Web! www.randomhouse.com/teens

Educators and librarians, for a variety of teaching tools,
visit us at www.randomhouse.com/teachers

The Library of Congress has cataloged the hardcover edition
of this work as follows:
Harmel, Kristin.
When you wish / Kristin Harmel.
p. cm.
Summary: When sixteen-year-old pop singing sensation Star Beck learns that her
father, who left when she was three, has been writing to her for six years, she
disguises herself, leaves her controlling mother and adoring fans behind, and
goes to find him—and, perhaps, a normal life—in St. Petersburg, Florida.
ISBN: 978-0-385-73475-2 (hardcover)—ISBN: 978-0-385-90474-2
(Gibraltar lib. bdg.)
[1. Fame—Fiction. 2. Singers—Fiction. 3. Popular music—Fiction. 4. Mothers and
daughters—Fiction. 5. Fathers and daughters—Fiction. 6. Saint Petersburg
(Fla.)—Fiction.] I. Title.
PZ7.H2116Whe 2008
[Fic]—dc22
2007020472

ISBN: 978-0-385-73592-6 (pbk.)
RL: 6.0
Printed in the United States of America
10 9 8 7 6 5 4 3 2 1
First Laurel-Leaf Edition

★

To my wonderful mom,
who has encouraged me,
supported me and inspired me
through everything

A huge thank-you:

To all the teachers who encouraged my writing, especially Mr. Dorsett, Mrs. Vann and Ms. Marcotte from Northeast High!

To my super editor, Wendy Loggia: Working with you is such a pleasure. You've helped me to grow so much as a writer, and I can never thank you enough for that.

To my fantastic agent, Jenny Bent; her lovely assistant, Victoria Horn; my awesome film agent, Andy Cohen; cover designer Marci Senders, editorial assistant Pam Bobowicz, and the whole Delacorte family.

To my great family, including Mom, Karen, Dave and Dad, and to all my wonderful friends, including three of my favorite teenagers: Cole, Carly and Luke Pearson.

To the best and most supportive writer friends in the world: Sarah Mlynowski (to whom I owe a great deal), Melissa Senate, Alison Pace and Lynda Curnyn, and to the talented fashion designer Amy Tangerine.

And to the three coolest rock stars I know: Ben Bledsoe, Courtney Jaye and Michael Ghegan. Star Beck's world would be a lot more fun if she could tour with you guys!

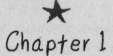

Chapter 1

I'm in the middle of a big photo shoot, and there's a fight going on about whether my bangs should be swept to the left or to the right. You would think that this decision is as important as, say, world peace or finding a cure for cancer.

Mariska (publicist): "Her best side is her right."

Don (hairstylist): "No, definitely left."

1

Marco Abruglio (the photographer): *"Pgfnht tfdsh gsdhtr! Cghtrehty!"* (Completely unintelligible yelps that I suspect are Italian curse words)

Mariska: "If her best side is her left, why did *Jane* shoot her right side?"

Don: "Why did *Seventeen* shoot her left?"

Unidentified fashion assistant: "Sweep her bangs back!"

Marco Abruglio: *"Pgfnht tfdsh gsdhtr! Pgfnht tfdsh gsdhtr!"*

Aimee (facialist): "She's getting a pimple on her forehead! Can't you see that? We must have the bangs!"

Mom (manager): "Can you pull the neckline down? Show a little more cleavage?"

Me: "Can't I just wear my bangs parted in the middle and swept to *both* sides?"

There's dead silence in the studio. All eyes turn to me. Everyone looks shocked that I have an opinion.

"Star?" my mother finally says, her voice as tight as her Botoxed forehead. "Why don't you just sit there and look pretty and let the adults handle this?"

I stare at her for a moment. All I can hear is the steady whir of the massive fan that's supposed to make me look windswept.

"Won't my bangs shift anyhow once I start moving?" I ask, glancing at the fan.

Again, silence.

"I'm not really used to the talent making demands," hisses Tiffini, the fashion director for *Dial* magazine. She turns and glares at Mariska. Then she smiles sweetly at me. "We'll do anything that makes you happy. You are, after all, the star!"

"Star, honey, why don't you just let us make a decision?" Mariska says. "You shouldn't really be concerning yourself with this."

I sigh. I look at her and then at Mom. I shoot death rays at Tiffini. I close my eyes.

"Fine," I mutter.

Everyone in the room goes back to squabbling. Should I have a flower in my hair, or a barrette? Should my lipstick be pale pink or nude? Peachy blush or rosy? Should my dress expose lots of cleavage or a little?

I'd like to say that I care. I'd like to tell you that I think I look prettier with pink lips and rosy blush. Or that I'd really prefer the barrette. But it's useless to have an opinion. You want to dress me up in a bikini with my hair back in a ponytail? Fine. An evening gown with an updo? Whatever. Heck, if Marco wanted to paint blue streaks up and down my face and dress me in a muumuu, I'd probably agree, as long as everyone stopped fighting about it. Which would never happen. My entourage *lives* to argue.

Actually, a muumuu might look better than what I'm wearing right now. Someone had the bright idea to debut the latest masterpiece from the House of Valerio (huge, crazy-expensive fashion designer in Italy) on me. Unfortunately, the House of Valerio's latest masterpiece just happens to be a frilly Pepto-Bismol-pink dress that I can't move in. And it's covered with ten thousand feathers.

I'm a giant pink chicken—yet everyone is concerned about my bangs.

Does this make any sense? Is anyone *really* going to be looking at the way my bangs are parted when the rest of me looks so ridiculous?

But I learned long ago that just because you're the pop star whose record-breaking career pays everyone's salaries doesn't actually mean that anyone listens to you at all.

Five hours later, with my blush (peach), my lipstick (nude), my bangs (swept to the right) and my outfit (hideous) replaced with my normal costume for the first set, I'm standing backstage at Madison Square Garden, waiting to go on for the second-to-last show of my *Simply Star* autumn tour.

"Star! Star! Star!" the audience begins to chant. My heart is racing, but it's not because of nerves. I never get nervous anymore. It's from the pure adrenaline, the pulse-pounding excitement of having twenty thousand fans screaming my name, singing the words to my songs, waving banners that read I LOVE YOU STAR! and wearing T-shirts with my face printed on them.

"You ready?" asks Ben, my spiky-haired guitar player, nudging me playfully in the shoulder with the neck of his Les Paul as we wait in the wings.

At 24, Ben is the only one of my band members who's even remotely close to my age (one of the guys is so old he could be my grandfather). He's like the big brother I never had.

Out in the arena, the roar of the crowd has reaching a deafening decibel. The opening band—the girl group Sistahs Three—has come and gone, and the audience is getting restless.

Ben winks at me as the guys all nod at each other and head out to their positions onstage. There's another roar from the crowd, more high-pitched screams. I wait thirty seconds for Dave to get his bass hooked up; Ben to adjust his guitar; Jay to settle in behind the keyboard; Casey, Michael and Al to get their horns tuned and Cash (the old guy) to slide in behind his immense drum kit. Then another thirty seconds for them to play the opening riffs. I close my eyes for a moment and let the roar of the crowd course through me. Then I begin my own trot out, smiling my big stage smile and waving my big stage wave before I even emerge from behind the curtains.

The roars and screams go up an octave as soon as I appear. I'm wearing a midriff-baring white tee, skintight gold, shimmery hot pants and gold, sparkly knee-high stiletto boots. Like every other night, I manage to dance in this because I've trained for years. (I could probably dance in a big clown suit if I had to—although I really hope my career never comes to that.)

Every time I bring my onstage wardrobe up with Mom, she instantly dismisses me. "You're crazy," she says, which seems to be her favorite word for me lately. "That's what your fans want to see you wear."

Okay, so maybe they do. But that doesn't mean *I'm* okay with it.

I have a body that I'm pretty confident about, thanks to my personal trainer, my dietician and two hours of dancing onstage each night. I just don't see why I'm expected to flaunt it *quite* this much.

"You know, normal moms try to get their daughters to dress *less* sluttily," I pointed out to her the last time I asked her why I couldn't perform in some less revealing clothes. Like maybe the cool cargo pants Fergie wears. Or the black pants and pretty dresses Kelly Clarkson gets to rock out in. But Mom just laughs.

"We've never been *normal*, Star," she says, wrinkling her nose like *normal* is a bad word. "You know that. You have to look perfect. You have to *be* perfect, Star."

"All I really want is you," I sing as I dance onto the stage, shielding my eyes for a moment against the glare of the spotlight and waving to the packed arena. A giant roar rises from the crowd again. Just as I hit the third line of the first verse, blindingly bright white fireworks shoot off from each end of the stage, and the audience collectively gasps. Two giant video monitors rise behind the band, and scenes from the video shoot for "You're the One" start pulsating to the tempo of the song.

I belt out the chorus. Kick-step. Kick-step. Shake butt. Jump-turn. Stage-wink at boy in audience. Kick-step. *"Even if you'll never love me. You're the one, you're the one. And it's breaking my heart to know."*

The lights dim slightly, more pyrotechnic flashes explode in time with the music, and the crowd screams at the top of their lungs.

While the band finishes the song and the crowd roars, I close my eyes for a second and breathe deeply, taking it all in. "Thank you all so much!" I yell into my microphone.

"You're a great crowd! I love . . . New York!" Another roar rises from the crowd, none of whom noticed, apparently, that I almost forgot where we are.

In the past seven days, we've played Philadelphia, D.C., Pittsburgh, Boston and now here, New York, the last stop of a thirty-city tour. It's really hard to keep track of where we are. I live in constant fear that I'll one day yell out the wrong city name and the audience will stare at me, like *What's* her *problem?*

But as my on-tour psychologist says, I probably worry too much about what other people think anyhow. And yes, I have an on-tour psychologist. Just one of Mom's many brilliant ideas.

The band starts playing the opening chords for "Fight Fire with Fire" while a giant torch rises from the center of the stage. Just as I start singing the first verse, an enormous flame erupts from the middle of the huge beacon, casting an eerie glow over the stage. The crowd goes wild; they always love all the dramatic staging stuff my tech guys do on tour. There are fireworks, crazy video displays, this huge torch and even a male model who rides onto stage on a white horse to literally sweep me off my feet during "Prince Charming," one of my biggest hits. The *Boston Herald*, the *L.A. Times* and the *New York Post* have all compared my stage show to Madonna's most recent over-the-top tour, and the *Chicago Tribune* even said that mine was more exciting.

Good thing, because it's almost $120 a ticket for the cheapest seat to see me play. That's why I begged Mom, Sarah and Mariska to see if we could tape an ABC concert special after this tour for people who couldn't afford to come. But as usual, I was outvoted. "You're so much more elite than broadcast television," Mom had cooed, apparently forgetting that Madonna herself had recently done a broadcast concert. No matter how famous I am, I seriously doubt that at sixteen, I can afford to be more elite than Madonna.

I launch into the "Fight Fire with Fire" chorus, tossing my waist-length curly red hair around the way my award-winning choreographer Lance Mojave taught me. I can almost hear his irritatingly squeaky voice in my head: *Oh yeah, work it girl.* My hair is my signature. It's the one thing everyone associates with me first. My mom once hired someone to do a focus group, and 82 percent of Americans checked the box marked "waist-length red hair" when asked to say what they thought of first when they thought of Star Beck. So cutting it is totally out of the question. According to my mom, at least. She promptly nixed my plans when I begged for a bob in July.

By the time the show ends, I'm out of breath, exhilarated

and starving. We do two encores, ending with the peppy, upbeat, Latin-flavored hit, "Your Love Is the Air I Breathe," a number-one single off my third album. It's the most complicated dance number of the whole show, and I'm backed up by two dozen dancers in brightly colored flamenco outfits. Fireworks explode all around us as I sing the last words. Then, with one final wave to the roaring crowd, I run offstage, while my band continues playing until the curtains go down.

When I get back to my dressing room, my grumbling stomach and I are a little disappointed to see only a basket of fruit, a veggie tray and six diet sodas. Not that this should be a surprise. A few years ago, when I'd toured with the boy band Six Degrees of Separation, those guys had a dressing room filled with candy bars, chips, sandwiches and every kind of soda you could imagine. But noooooo. Not my dressing room. Mom always makes sure to explicitly request that my dressing room at each venue be stocked only with "healthy, calorie-conscious options." Yuck.

"You don't want to get tubby," my mom says, as if reading my hungry mind, coming into the room behind me, dressed in a flowy white designer dress, her blond hair done up in a tight twist and her makeup thick and dark. She kisses me on the cheek and then swats me lightly on the butt. "No one likes a fat pop star," she adds cheerfully.

"Right," I mutter. I reach resignedly for a celery stick and a can of Diet Sprite.

Yeah. As if a few M&Ms would make me fat after I've spent almost two hours dancing under 120-degree klieg lights. But I live in a diet dictatorship run by my mom.

"Off to bed within an hour, Star," she says sternly after I've eaten three more celery sticks, a carrot and a piece of cauliflower. Did I mention she threw out the ranch dip too? Seriously, I can see it in the trash can. She can be really cruel sometimes. "You have your date with Jesse tomorrow. You want to be *on*."

"Yeah," I say glumly. "Heaven forbid everything not be *perfect*."

★

Chapter 2

I love my mom, but we don't exactly have a typical mother-daughter relationship. Most sixteen-year-olds work a part-time job or get an allowance from their parents. I work full-time while my mom sits around in spas and hotel suites and lawyers' offices all day. She controls me and my money because I'm only a minor and she's my guardian.

But here's the funny thing. People think my life is perfect because I'm a famous pop star. And sure, life's different. I basically live in five-star hotels. I know how to drive, but I don't have a car because I spend most of my life being chauffeured around in limousines. I support my mother with my earnings and haven't seen the inside of a classroom since I was ten (a tutor toured with us until my sixteenth birthday, when I took the GED and was pronounced a high school graduate). I don't have to worry about being popular, and I don't have to apply to colleges (even though I kind of want to go to one someday), because I've already made gabillions of dollars.

But just like most other teenagers, I fight with my mom. All the time.

No, scratch that. Not *all* the time. I can't even *find* her most of the time. Most of the time, she's out getting her nails done or her hair dyed or her face poked and prodded, or she's meeting with publicists and lawyers and trying to sign endorsement deals for cosmetics or jeans or books or whatever she happens to be into that week.

And you have to actually be able to locate someone in order to fight with them, don't you? Sometimes I think I'd prefer the constant fighting, because at least it would mean I'd get to talk with her.

You name it, we've argued about it. My hair. My complete lack of days off ("Slacking off isn't going to win you another Grammy," she always says.) My slutty stage out-fits. Even boys. Not that there *are* boys to fight about. Contrary to what the tabloids say, I've never even had a *real* first kiss. Really, I'm utterly, pathetically clueless when it comes to guys (despite several kissing scenes in music videos and the few movies I've starred in). But Mom is al-ways insisting that I have to act like I have all sorts of expe-rience.

"Girls look up to you," she says. "They want to *be* you. No one aspires to be innocent anymore. And the second they find out you are, well, they'll think you're a loser."

Thanks, Mom.

Sure, fame, fans, money and all the other perks of being a pop star make some things easier. And yeah, it's awesome to be called "the next pop queen" by *Entertainment Weekly* and "America's favorite teenager" by *Teen Vogue*. But I'm alone all the time, I don't have any friends, I haven't had a decent conversation with my own mother in more than two years. And a boyfriend? Forget it.

Who'd want a life like that?

Fortunately, when you're famous, the money and atten-tion that cause you problems can also solve some of them. And that's where Jesse Bishop comes in.

If I'm the most famous female teen pop star in America, Jesse Bishop is my male equivalent. We've known each other forever. We costarred on *Family Business*, and later, he guest-starred on my Disney Channel show, *Secrets of My Teenage Life*. We took acting lessons together when we were six, right after I got my first big break, which means that I've know him longer than pretty much anyone else in the industry.

As far as America knows, I've been dating Jesse for the last two months. The truth is, although he's a nice guy, it's made my skin crawl each of the six times he's kissed me (which were all in front of dozens of cameras), because I don't have romantic feelings for him. That and, well, he's just a really bad kisser. Not that I have much to compare him to, but I am pretty sure that your lips aren't supposed to hurt after you finish making out with someone. I'm also pretty sure that I've never seen anyone's teeth smashing awkwardly together in any kissing scenes in movies.

I'm guessing that Jesse probably never *had* to learn to kiss right. He's always making out with random fans. His manager encourages it (Jesse has a bad-boy image to maintain). Most girls are probably so thrilled to make out with him that it's not like they'd stop in the middle and say, "You're really bad at this."

Bad kissing aside, Jesse is undeniably hot, with his

floppy, sun-streaked surfer hair, his dimples and his broad shoulders. His management team has done an amazing job of creating a mystique around him; he's always slightly evasive in interviews, and instead of answering personal questions, he just arches his eyebrow at the camera and winks one of his beautiful green eyes, and girls swoon. I'm not kidding; I've seen girls faint.

It doesn't hurt that his last three singles—two dance hits and a romantic ballad—hit number one. He's in *People* almost every week and is a frequent *TRL* guest host.

So when our publicists and managers cooked up a little fake romance to help promote our most recent CDs, which launched within two weeks of each other, I went along with it. I mean, don't get me wrong, I actually *do* like Jesse. Aside from Ben, he's one of my only friends. He's one of the people who really, truly understand the weirdness of my life. But kissing him is all gnashed teeth and slobbery wetness. Holding his clammy palm always makes me squirm. And even looking into those theoretically dreamy eyes makes me want to hurl, because honestly, I've known him for so long that he feels as much like my brother as Ben does. And who would want to gaze into their brother's eyes? Ick.

But when you're the most famous teen pop star in America, it really doesn't matter what *you* want. If your mom and your publicist and your manager and everyone else in your professional life agree that you're dating Jesse Bishop, well then, you're dating Jesse Bishop.

And when the whole world thinks you're dating Jesse Bishop, it makes it a lot easier to escape the fact that in reality, you're sixteen and haven't even had a *real* first kiss. That in reality, for all your fame and popularity, you're a Loser with a capital *L*.

That's how my loserific self ended up in Battery Park on the southern tip of Manhattan the day after my first Madison Square Garden show. My mom, Mariska and Jesse's publicist agreed that we'd meet there and stroll through the park so the media pool following us could get lots of great patriotic shots of us checking out the Korean War memorial with the Statue of Liberty across the water in the background. The whole story—with our wildly patriotic selves—is sure to get picked up by all the newspapers, magazines and TV shows because we hardly ever appear in public together. It will look like we're just out doing normal, everyday stuff like normal, everyday people. Our publicists love to have us do "normal" stuff because it makes us seem more accessible to the public and easier to identify with.

Actual normal stuff—like letting the press see my mom yelling at me? Or trying to sneak out to go out with Ben and his friends (I say "trying" because I always get caught by a bodyguard)? Or arguing about what time I have to go to bed? Not allowed.

As Jesse takes my hand and we start strolling from the World War II memorial toward the ferry docks, it's hard to ignore the fact that there's an entourage of nearly thirty people scurrying behind us, as well as a handful of bodyguards to keep the curious crowds away. It isn't exactly your normal, everyday romantic walk in the park when you're being followed by your mother; your faux boyfriend's parents; your personal publicists and the publicist for your faux boyfriend's record label; cameramen for *Extra, Entertainment Tonight,* CNN's *Showbiz Tonight* and ABC; photogs for *Us Weekly,* the *New York Times,* the *Boston Globe,* and the Associated Press; the authors of *HOT: The Unauthorized Biography of Jesse Bishop* and *POP! The Unauthorized Biography of Star Beck* and a dozen scribbling reporters.

"So how's everything?" Jesse asks under his breath with his signature charmingly lopsided grin as we casually stroll. "Are you still locked in a battle with the Queen of All Evil?"

"*Toss the hair, toss the hair!*" Mariska hisses from

somewhere behind us. I sigh and obey. Every flashbulb goes off at once.

"Is that your latest nickname for my mother?" I whisper.

"Your mother?" Jesse feigns innocence. "Why, that would make you the spawn of the devil!"

"Jesse!" I exclaim, punching him in the arm. "She's not *that* bad." *I* can talk badly about my mom. But it's not like I want Jesse to. "I mean, she took me shopping the other day in Boston, you know," I say, realizing how defensive I sound. "We spent the whole afternoon together."

There. That's nice mother-daughter behavior, right?

"Wow," Jesse says. He looks sidelong at me and rolls his eyes. "How many necklaces did she buy? And how many reporters were along to see you 'bonding'?"

Okay, I don't want to talk about this anymore. We pass a gaggle of screaming little girls wearing Jesse Bishop tees. He waves halfheartedly. I take a deep breath and paste on a smile. "So. How are *you* doing?" I ask. Jesse's favorite subject is, and always has been, Jesse.

His face brightens. "Same," Jesse says. He sighs dramatically, shakes his head and looks down at me. "Busy. Crazy. Every day a new city. Every city, different girls."

This is so typical of him.

"Aren't they jealous of your girlfriend, Star Beck?" I tease. I know it should bother me that he's out there hooking up with girls while the whole world thinks he's dating me.

19

After all, my faux boyfriend is faux cheating on me. But I just think it's sort of funny.

"I think they like it," he says, grinning wickedly. "They're thrilled they're getting their hands on Star Beck's man. Sick, huh?"

"You're terrible," I mutter.

We stroll a bit more in near silence, with Jesse pointing and faking deep interest in the Statue of Liberty and photographers nudging to the front of the entourage to take pictures.

"So you're doing an interview with *Dial* magazine tomorrow?" Jesse asks as I try to control my hair, which is now blowing wildly in the breeze. More flashbulbs go off around us. Apparently my hair blowing constitutes a potential Pulitzer Prize–winning moment for these photogs. "Your publicist's assistant told my agent, who told my publicist, who told my mom," he adds. I roll my eyes. "Yeah, I'm doing *Dial*," I say. "No big deal."

"No big deal?" he repeats with a bit of a smirk.

"Shut up," I grumble. Jesse's smart enough to stop talking. He knows just as well as Mom and Mariska do that I hate interviews. For one big reason.

When someone's doing a feature on me, they always want to know about my dad. That's because my father walked out on my mom and me. Reporters want me to cry and say all sorts of dramatic things, but the truth is, he left when I was three and we moved on. Mom shortened my name from Amanda Star Beckendale-Mecham to Star Beck. I got famous. End of story. What's the big deal, right?

But really—not that I would ever tell a reporter this—it is a little bit of a big deal. To me, at least. It's not like I can just totally forget about the father who simply disappeared one day.

The more frustrated I get with all the stupid "rules" of being famous, the more I find myself wondering what really happened to the "normal" dad I never had a chance to know.

Not that I'll ever have a chance to find out.

"Just forget about him, Star," Mom always snaps. I might as well.

"Ready?" Jesse asks. We've reached the railing between two ferry docks, where we're to share a "spontaneous" kiss for the cameras. The Statue of Liberty is framed perfectly behind us.

I sigh. "Lay one on me, stud." Jesse laughs and leans down to kiss me.

This is just as fake and staged as everything else in my life. *Everything*. I can't think of a single thing about me that's real anymore. It's like I've been swept up in a tide of lies, and everyone is in on it but me. I'm having more and more trouble coming up for air.

But I kiss back anyhow. I don't really have a choice, do I?

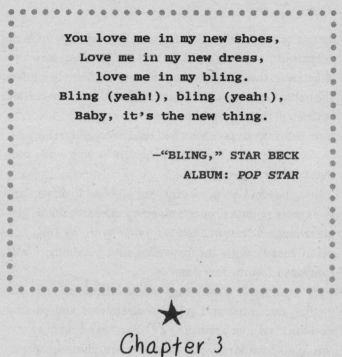

> You love me in my new shoes,
> Love me in my new dress,
> love me in my bling.
> Bling (yeah!), bling (yeah!),
> Baby, it's the new thing.
>
> —"BLING," STAR BECK
> ALBUM: *POP STAR*

★

Chapter 3

I used to think that the best thing about being famous was that everyone would know me—my name, my face, my music. Then reality set in.

After several years of working really hard-to-score roles on Nickelodeon shows and Disney sitcoms, I finally made it big. I would walk into hotel rooms when I was first touring with Six Degrees of Separation, and there would be dozens of white lilies (my favorite flower), bags of York Peppermint Patties (my favorite candy), piles of white teddy bears (modeled after my character's favorite stuffed animal on *Secrets of My Teenage Life*) and dozens of bottles of Clean perfume (my favorite scent) waiting for me, gifts from overzealous fans who had read every magazine article I'd ever been featured in. I thought it was really cool that my fans *knew* me.

Sure, they had never met me. But all I had to do was answer some reporters' questions every once in a while, giggle through a *Tonight Show* interview with Jay Leno and make friends with the paparazzi and suddenly, I was everyone's favorite pop star.

But it's not like it was easy. While other kids were out playing freeze tag and going to sleepovers and passing notes in class, I was pursuing a career. Spending pilot season in L.A., working with vocal coaches, choreographers, dance instructors, personal trainers, guitar teachers, acting coaches, and media trainers. It was a full-time job.

And it paid off.

I was in my first touring musical by the time I was six and had guest spots on soap operas by eight. At nine, I scored a small role in an M. Night Shyamalan movie and landed the *Family Business* gig, and at ten, I was cast in the lead role in *Secrets of My Teenage Life*. After three years on the show, I recorded my debut pop album, and the first single hit number three on the Billboard charts within two weeks of its release. We released my second album right after I turned fourteen, the same year *Secrets of My Teenage Life* went off the air after a great four-year run, and we decided to focus on my music career.

Two years later? I have two Grammys and every one of my five albums has sold over a million copies. I sell out stadium shows all over the world, and "my people" are constantly fielding film offers, potential music collaborations and endorsement deals. I like it, for the most part. But sometimes it would be nice to be normal, although I have no idea what "normal" would really feel like.

I guess I'll never know.

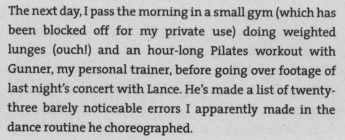

The next day, I pass the morning in a small gym (which has been blocked off for my private use) doing weighted lunges (ouch!) and an hour-long Pilates workout with Gunner, my personal trainer, before going over footage of last night's concert with Lance. He's made a list of twenty-three barely noticeable errors I apparently made in the dance routine he choreographed.

"Honestly, Star, are you going to take this seriously or not?" he asks, letting out a disturbed sigh.

I'm torn between hating him and feeling frustrated that I'm not getting it right. It's not like I'm not trying. But nothing I do is good enough for him.

"You're never going to reach the next level if you don't want it," he snaps.

"I want it," I mumble back.

"Then you need to work harder." He rolls his eyes at me. "Some days, I don't know how you got to be the pop princess you are."

Mom lets him talk to me like this only because he's the best in the business. I'm not even allowed to snap back. I bite my tongue so hard it hurts.

I'm mentally and physically exhausted by the time I head back to the Regency on Park Avenue with Mike and Tiny Joe, my bodyguards. The lobby is overflowing with screaming fans holding I LOVE STAR and YOU'RE THE STAR OF MY WORLD banners as I cut across to the elevators. I stop and sign a few dozen autographs. (I'm allowed to sign in "controlled environments," like hotel lobbies, when I have two or more bodyguards present.)

"We love you!" gush two little girls in unison as I sign a white canvas teddy bear with the pink Sharpie they've handed me.

"You're pretty great too," I say, winking at them, trying to ignore the fact that my legs are killing me, thanks to my dance practice with Lance. I'm starting to get a splitting headache. One girl shrieks so loudly that I'm afraid my cardrums are about to pop. This does not help my headache.

"W-would you g-go out with me?" asks a boy who can't be older than ten, as I sign a poster he hands me. I smile at him.

"I wish I could," I say. "But you know, Jesse Bishop might get mad." It's times like this that my faux romance comes in handy.

"He d-doesn't l-love you as much as I do," the boy says solemnly, his voice cracking. "My dad could drive us to the m-movies."

"Ask me again in a few years," I say. I give him a peck on the cheek and he turns beet red.

"You're hot," says a teenage boy dressed all in black as he thrusts a CD case at me for my autograph.

"You totally rule," affirms a pink-cheeked girl in a T-shirt emblazoned with my last album cover.

"Totally," agrees her redheaded friend, who's decked out in a *Simply Star* tee. Her head bobs up and down in an endless enthusiastic nod as she grins at me.

By the time I step into the elevator, I'm even more exhausted. I can feel the smile melt from my face. I slump back against the wall and close my eyes.

"You don't have to do that, you know," Mike says. I think for a minute and crack my eyes open.

"Yeah, I do," I answer. "All those people have been waiting down there just to catch a glimpse of me. It's crazy. But look how happy it makes them if I stop for a minute. How can I not?"

I step out of the elevator on the penthouse floor (with Mike and Tiny Joe tailing me, of course) and slide my key card into the door of the enormous suite I'm sharing with Mom. Inside, she's flitting from room to room, humming to herself as she glances at her reflection in each of the many mirrors that hang on different walls. She has already changed from the Juicy sweats she was wearing earlier into a simple black dress. Her neck is draped with pearls.

"Honey, I'm going to have Don do my hair, then I need you to meet me in his suite on the eleventh floor in forty-five minutes," she says without really looking at me. "You and I are going shopping!"

I pause in the doorway and stare at her.

"Is it just me and you this time?" I ask suspiciously. "Or is this another media op?"

What I didn't tell Jesse earlier was that he was right: on our mother-daughter shopping trip in Boston a couple of days ago, Mom invited along at least a dozen reporters. Not exactly cozy bonding time.

Mom smiles innocently.

"It's just some mother-daughter time, princess." She

absently crosses the room and gives me a peck on the cheek. "I don't get to see enough of my little girl."

She spritzes some Chanel No. 5 perfume on her neck, on her wrists and over the front of her dress; then she glides toward the door, air-kisses me on both cheeks from about a foot away and leaves, chirping over her shoulder, "See you in an hour, sweet pea!"

After she's gone, I sigh, walk into the smaller bedroom of the suite and flop onto the king-sized bed that is my home away from home for the second night in a row. At least I'll have a few minutes to relax before venturing out in public again.

Just as I close my eyes and start to unwind, there's a knock on my door.

"Star!" comes a frantic voice. I sit up. "Star? It's Melissa. Are you there? Let me in if you're there. Your mom wanted me to go over some outfit choices with you."

I close my eyes for a minute and try to center myself. Okay, so apparently this mother-daughter day is important enough that Mom has sent my stylist to dress me. I guess flip-flops and jeans aren't good enough, even when the flip-flops are Juicy and the jeans are Swarovski-studded Sevens.

"Coming," I shout halfheartedly. I drag myself away from the beckoning bed and make my way to the front door.

"Star, Star, Star!" Melissa, a punkish woman in her thirties with pink-streaked black hair gushes at me from the hallway. She's pushing a long rolling rack of clothes. "Omigod. We have, like, thirty minutes. We have to hurry!"

An hour and a half later, Mom and I are standing in the famous Tiffany store on Fifth Avenue, looking at bracelets and rings presented to us on little pale blue pillows by two grinning salesmen and a blushing saleswoman who are entirely ignoring the other customers in the store. In all fairness, though, I've noticed that the other customers aren't really looking at the jewelry anyhow; they're watching me. As usual, I try to pretend I don't notice. Mike and Tiny Joe try to blend into the woodwork as well as two six-foot-five-inch-tall linebacker-sized men can.

Melissa has decked me out in a little Dolce & Gabbana silver and gold lame dress, which seems awfully fancy for a late-morning shopping trip. But she's managed to dress it down with opaque black tights, casual black ballet flats and some chunky gold jewelry. Mom is still wearing her black cocktail dress and pearls, and Don has blown out her hair perfectly, as usual.

"Ooh, Star, this one is *so* pretty," Mom gushes, holding up a silver-beaded bracelet. I nod and she turns to one of the salesmen. "How much?"

"One hundred fifty," the man says after checking the price. Mom frowns.

"That's all? Could we see something more expensive?"

I roll my eyes as the salespeople present Mom with an array of other options: shiny cocktails rings, charm necklaces, pins. Finally, the saleswoman appears with a bracelet that makes Mom's eyes light up.

"Ooh, honey, it's little stars!" she exclaims.

I look at the bracelet, which is, admittedly, pretty.

"It's nice," I say.

"Stars!" she repeats loudly, in case I didn't get it the first time. "Like your name! Star!"

I look at her strangely. Does she think I'm a total idiot?

"I know, Mom," I say.

Mom reaches for the bracelet, and the salespeople rush to help her clasp it on her wrist. She turns it over and smiles as the little diamond star charms catch the light.

"That's our Tiffany Star charm bracelet," explains one of the salesmen. "Just under a carat's worth of diamonds. Fifty-two hundred dollars."

"Fifty-two hundred? Excellent! We'll take it!" Mom exclaims instantly, still admiring the way it sparkles on her wrist.

"Wonderful," says the salesman smoothly. He's probably mentally calculating his commission. "Shall I wrap it up for Star?"

Mom looks at him blankly.

"My daughter? No, this is for me," she says. She glances at me, then smiles sweetly at the sales staff. "This way I can always keep Star close."

"Awwww," the salespeople say in unison.

I smile tightly and wonder how long it will take for that quote to get into *Us Weekly*.

An hour and a half later, we're sitting down at a fancy French restaurant off Fifth Avenue for lunch. I'm feeling a bit better. After Mom's Tiffany purchase, we actually bonded a bit at Bergdorf Goodman, Bulgari and the Manolo Blahnik store on West Fifty-fourth, where Mom picked out four pairs of shoes.

"I'll have the roast duck, but leave the orange peel out of the glaze and substitute Splenda for the sugar," Mom rattles off to our waiter. "Steamed broccoli instead of the asparagus, with just a touch of lemon, but don't oversteam the florets or I'll send them back. Rice instead of the potato, but make it jasmine rice with a hint of ginger. And the house salad, dressing on the side, no mushrooms, extra tomatoes."

The waiter jots down Mom's detailed order, looking panicked. Then he turns to me.

"Um, Miss Beck?" he asks, sounding sort of nervous. I glance around, and as usual, the entire restaurant seems to be staring at us. I can hear the whispers and murmurs that follow me wherever I go.

"I'll have a cheeseburger and a Coke, please," I say, wondering if Mom will notice. Of course she does.

"You will not!" she exclaims indignantly. The waiter pauses halfway through writing the words.

"Mom, I—" I begin.

"Star!" she cuts me off, keeping her voice low. "Remember yourself!" Before I can protest, she turns to the waiter and chirps, "She'll have the Caesar salad with your fat-free Caesar dressing. Hold the Parmesan cheese, hold the croutons."

"So, uh, just lettuce with fat-free dressing?" the waiter clarifies.

"Dressing on the side," Mom commands.

The waiter nods and scurries away.

"I didn't *want* a Caesar salad," I say.

"You have *Dial* in two hours" is what she tells me.

Fine. Okay. Deep breaths. I can eat a Caesar salad.

"We should do this more often," I say tentatively once her

33

meal and my lettuce arrive. "Do things just the two of us. It's nice."

And it is. Even with my mom being pretty high maintenance and spending more money in two hours than most people make in six months of work, it's been a nice day. After all, getting to spend time alone with her is a rare thing.

"I'm kind of nervous about my interview," I blurt out in this rare moment of mother-daughter bonding. "I hate it when they ask me about Dad."

Mom stops chewing and looks at me sharply.

"Star," she begins. She shakes her head. "Honey, you have to deal with that. It's always going to come up. Just remember, it's not *your* fault your father walked out on you. On us, I mean. And besides, it made you who you are today. Remember?" She lowers her voice. "We've rehearsed this a million times, Star."

Of course I remember. It's one of the lines I'm expected to say whenever a reporter asks about how my dad's leaving shaped my life. *It made me who I am today,* I always say slowly, thoughtfully. *That which doesn't break us makes us stronger.* If they press on and say, *But did it hurt you? Do you miss him?* I sadly say, *I never really had the chance to know him. It's always been my mom and me, as long as I can remember.*

But the thing is, I don't really mean it.

34

I *do* remember my dad. A little, at least. Just bits and pieces, really—foggy images of playing ring-around-the-rosy with him or of him waiting at the bottom of a playground slide to catch me. I have vague memories of him tucking me in at night and singing me to sleep with Beatles songs from the sixties. I *don't* remember him seeming like he wanted to leave.

But what did I know? I was only three.

"Honey, you really have to nail this interview," Mom says, clearly already done with the subject of my father. "The cover of *Dial* is a big deal."

"I know." Of course I know. I know how this whole thing works.

"Good," Mom says. She takes another bite of duck. I watch her jealously. Her meal looks way better than mine. "I just want you to know how much I love you, honey. Really. Being your mother is such a gift."

A leaf of lettuce actually falls out of my mouth. She's staring at me with wide blue eyes, a gentle expression on her face. For a moment, I wonder if I heard her wrong. I can't even remember the last time my mom said "I love you" to me, and suddenly she's pouring out her heart? I glance around suspiciously, wondering if there are reporters nearby, but although people around the restaurant are staring at us (which I'm so accustomed to I hardly notice anymore), the diners within earshot all seem absorbed in their own conversations. Unbelievably, Mom actually seems to be saying something kind to me for real.

"I . . . I love you too, Mom," I respond shakily, still totally caught off guard.

"We make a good team, don't we?" she says, beaming at me. "Just you and me, against the world."

"Um, yeah," I say, confused by her sudden and unexpected display of emotion. Mom reaches across the table and grasps my hand. I notice her palm is sweaty.

"We couldn't have made it this far without each other," she continues, staring into my eyes. I blink at her, not sure what to say. I mean, I guess it's true. I couldn't have become a pop star if she hadn't pushed me into it. And she couldn't have become a richer-than-God woman if I hadn't become a pop star.

"I really love you, honey," Mom continues. I stare at her for a moment and realize that it's the first time I've heard her say that with no ulterior motive for years.

"I know, Mom," I say, taking a bite of my lettuce. I chew slowly and swallow. "I love you too."

But I can't shake the sense that something isn't quite right.

Are you satisfied
Now that you've done what you've
done?
Can you look me in the eye
Now that it's all come undone?

—"UNDONE," STAR BECK
ALBUM: *SECRETS OF A STAR*

★

Chapter 4

After our late lunch, I change into my favorite pink track pants and a matching hoodie, put my hair in a ponytail (despite Don's horrified protests—"I spent an hour on that hair!") and sit down with Karen Davidson, the *Dial* reporter, in a suite on the second floor of our hotel.

"You look familiar," I tell her after we shake hands. Mariska has settled into a chair in the corner to observe the interview, as usual.

"I don't believe we've ever met," Karen says, furrowing her forehead. Well, who can blame me? These reporters all start looking the same after a while.

She launches into her interview questions, which are all pretty standard. "How have you felt about this tour? Tell us about your next album. Has life changed since you won two Grammys last year? Are you and Jesse Bishop still going strong as pop's 'it' couple?"

I answer politely, my words well rehearsed. No questions about my dad so far. Everything is fine.

Then, a half hour into the interview, Karen gets a call on her cell.

"Oh no! You're kidding!" she says into the phone, her face shocked. She glances at Mariska and puts her hand over the receiver. "My editor says there's some problem with photo permissions. If we don't work it out right now, we won't be able to run Star on the cover. Can you handle this?"

Lose the cover? Mariska grabs the phone and nods.

"Hello?" she says before mouthing, *I'll be back in a minute* to me. Then she steps outside the interview room, leaving Karen and me alone.

The moment the door has shut behind Mariska, Karen turns back to me. "So you and your mom have a very close relationship?" she prompts, leaning forward eagerly.

"Sure." I shrug.

"In fact, she said just today that 'being your mother is such a gift,'" Karen continues.

"You interviewed my mom today?" I ask, wondering why she didn't mention it to me.

"No, no, she said it to you over lunch," Karen says brightly.

"What?"

"It's right here," Karen pulls a tape recorder from her purse. I stare at it. She presses Play.

"Being your mother is such a gift." I hear Mom's tinny voice from the recorder.

"I . . . I love you too, Mom," my voice responds. I suck in a breath. I reach out and push the Stop button on the recorder before I have to listen to any more of our talk.

"That was a private conversation!" I exclaim. Karen looks surprised.

"But your mother invited us along," she says, looking at me blankly. "We were at the next table over. I thought you knew."

"You were at Tiffany too," I say as it suddenly dawns on me why she looks familiar. She nods.

"And Bergdorf. . . . My mother invited you?" I can't believe it.

"And offered to wear a wire so we could record your whole day together," Karen chirps. She claps happily and leans forward again. "It will make a great opener for the magazine piece. '*Dial* is invited along exclusively on Star Beck's mother-daughter day!'"

"But . . . ," I start to protest, but the reporter has already switched gears.

"So is it true that Jack and Jill paid you thirty thousand dollars to wear their shoes in your photo shoot yesterday?" Karen asks.

"What?" Where is Mariska when I need her? "No!"

"Or that you received two hundred fifty thousand dollars last month for those 'candid' shots of you drinking a can of Diet Melonball soda?"

"No!" I'm feeling dizzy. I don't even *like* Melonball soda; it's just what I was handed when I said I was thirsty.

"Or that your mother has been in talks with preeminent plastic surgeon Richard Wrigley to discuss your nose job?"

"What?" I reach up, startled, and touch my nose. I like my nose! "No! I'm not getting a nose job."

Karen narrows her eyes. "*Dial* has also learned that even though you've said in numerous interviews that your father left you, in fact, it's *you* who have been shutting him out of *your* life since you've become famous, presumably to keep him away from your fortune," she says.

I can feel my heart stop for a minute. My jaw drops.

"What?" I squeak incredulously. The reporter smiles triumphantly. She's obviously thrilled to have gotten a reaction out of me.

"We have proof," she says. She looks so gleeful I'm afraid she's about to get up and start dancing a jig.

"Huh? What proof?" I'm lost. This can't be happening. She's obviously lying.

"Is it true?" she continues, ignoring my question. "Have you been lying to the media all these years, making up some sob story about your dad abandoning you just to get sympathy?"

I can't breathe. "Listen, that's enough," I say, trying to sound confident. "This interview is over!"

Karen continues like I haven't said anything at all. "When all along it was your mother who took you away from him?"

"That's not what happened!" I retort. My heart is racing. "You've been seriously misinformed."

I start to stand up, fully intending to walk away. But the reporter just smiles calmly.

"That's hard for you to say when I have proof right here," she says, holding up an envelope. I stop in my tracks for a moment, unable to tear my eyes away from it. Then I lean forward, despite myself, and stare. It's addressed to me but under my real name, Amanda Star Beckendale-Mecham.

And in the upper left corner, above an unfamiliar address in St. Petersburg, Florida, is a very familiar name.

Peter Mecham.

My dad.

I take the letter from her. Just then, Mariska reenters the room. Her face registers surprise the moment she sees me standing there looking like I've seen a ghost.

"Star? You okay?" she asks.

But I'm already breezing past her and the smirking reporter, on my way out the door, shaking so hard I feel like I'm in the middle of an earthquake.

I slam the door to my hotel suite behind me and sit down on the floor right there to tear the letter open.

> Dear Amanda,
>   Maybe it's crazy that I'm still writing to you after all this time. But I just want you to know that I've never forgotten about you. You must have a good reason for not wanting to talk with me, but I would give the world to speak with you again. You are——and always will be—— my little girl.
>
>   Love,
>   Daddy

I read the letter over twice. Then a sudden wave of nausea hits me. I make it into the bathroom just in time to throw up.

I can't find Mom anywhere. She's not in our suite. She's not in the hotel spa. Her cell goes straight to voice mail.

Mariska is at my door within five minutes.

"Star?" She pounds on the door loudly. "Star? I know you're in there. Open up."

"Go away!" I finally yell. I wipe my mouth on a towel in the bathroom, swish some water around in my mouth, spit and wipe again.

"Star, open the door!" she insists. I ignore her, but she keeps pounding.

Finally, I cross the room and yank open the door.

"What?" I demand.

"Star," she begins. She pauses, like she doesn't know what to say next. She stands there for a moment and takes me in. I know I must look like a wreck. Red-rimmed eyes. Pale, lifeless skin. I probably smell a little like vomit.

"What do you want?"

"I . . ." Her voice trails off. "Can I come in?"

"Whatever." I shrug and slouch away from the door. I feel like I'm walking through fog. The words from the letter keep replaying themselves in my mind. I keep trying to remind myself that the letter could be a fake. The reporter could just be trying to get a reaction out of me. But there's something about the smug, triumphant way she smiled at me that makes my blood run cold. Somehow, I know she's not lying.

And if the letter is real, I don't even know where to begin.

"Star," Mariska starts again, following me into the suite. I sit down on the couch and she sits tentatively across from me. There's a moment of silence. I feel numb. "Star," she finally starts again. "About the letter . . ."

"Is it real?" I ask. I finally look at her. She hesitates. Just long enough for me to know the answer. After a moment, she nods.

"Yes."

"How did that reporter get it?" I pick up the letter, which I've put back in its envelope, and look at it. Again, Mariska hesitates.

"An intern," she finally says. I just look at her. She continues, her voice heavy. "As you can see, it was sent to you in care of your management company. Every summer, they have college interns working, and apparently this summer, one of the interns stole the letter and gave it to *Dial*."

"This can't be happening," I mumble.

"Don't worry," Mariska says quickly. "I'm doing damage control. We're slapping them with a lawsuit, and we're even trying to get the federal government involved since it includes tampering with mail that was addressed to you."

"But that isn't going to stop them, is it?" I ask. Mariska hesitates, then shakes her head.

"Honestly?" she says. "Probably not. This is a big story for them, you know."

I'm silent for a moment. It feels like I've been punched in the stomach.

"Mariska," I say slowly. I look her right in the eye. "Do you know anything about my dad?"

I can't even believe I'm asking, after thirteen years of being silenced every time I bring him up to my mom. Is it possible Mariska has had some real answers all along?

She pauses.

"Yes," she says finally. "Your mother asked a private detective to look into him last year."

"What?" I ask. Mariska nods slowly.

"It was after . . . one of his letters," she says haltingly.

"*One* of his letters?" I repeat, feeling sick again. Mariska looks away.

"He lives in St. Petersburg, Florida," Mariska says flatly. "He owns a music store called Mecham's Music. He had just filed for bankruptcy at the time."

My heart feels heavy. I can't quite absorb it all. The fact that my dad owns a music store makes me feel buoyant and depressed at the same time. We obviously have something in common—which makes me feel good in a strange way.

"So this isn't the first letter my father has sent me?"

Mariska hesitates, then shakes her head.

"No," she says. She looks up and meets my eye. "He's been writing to you once a month for the last six years."

> I'm gonna dance my last dance,
> I'm gonna sing my last song,
> I'm gonna throw out my high heels
> And put
> my blue jeans on.
>
> —"MY BLUE JEANS," STAR BECK
> ALBUM: *SIMPLY STAR*

★

Chapter 5

*D*ave, my bass player, scoops me up in his arms and gives me loud kisses on both cheeks. It's the last night of the tour, so the mood is particularly cheerful backstage. My band guys, of course, have no idea anything is wrong. Thanks to years in the spotlight, I'm great at putting on a happy face.

"You're our little Super Star!" Dave exclaims. Everyone

47

laughs. The guys have a week off before we hit the recording studio to start laying down tracks for the next album, which will be released in February. I'll have the week off the road, but of course I won't actually be *off*. Lance Mojave will be working me to death on the dance moves he wants me to learn for the video for the first single off the album, which we haven't even recorded yet.

"You okay, Star?" Ben whispers in my ear.

"I'm fine."

"No, you're not," he says. "Something's wrong."

"I'm fine," I repeat. Ben looks at me for a long moment.

"You sure you don't want to talk about it?" he asks.

"I'm sure." I shake my head.

"Well, whenever you do, you know where to find me."

"I know," I say.

Now if I only knew where to find myself.

I don't see Mom backstage. That's typical. When the show is over, she usually gets the limo to take her back to the hotel so that she's already showered, waiting and watching TV in bed or preparing to go out for drinks when I get back. But tonight, I have a sneaking suspicion that Mariska told her what happened and she's avoiding me.

I eat a small snack of carrots, celery and mango slices and change into my street clothes—faded jeans, a black Amy Tangerine HAPPINESS T-shirt, black and white Pumas and a pink Dodgers baseball cap. I walk outside to tell Mike and Tiny Joe that I'm ready to go.

The limo takes me back to the Regency, where my whole entourage will stay tonight before taking a noon flight back to Los Angeles tomorrow. We came east by tour bus, slowly hitting all the major cities in the West and Midwest, but it would take days to retrace the same route home. Instead, the two tour bus drivers and the equipment truck driver will drive back on their own and meet us in L.A.

During my concert tonight, I managed to push aside most of my feelings, but now they all come flooding back. I'm so upset by the time we arrive at the Regency that I don't even stop and sign autographs in the lobby. I feel bad about it as the fans gaze after me with crushed expressions, but I can't handle it tonight.

I take the elevator straight up to the suite, looking forward to a little privacy. Even though I know I need to have it out with her, I kind of hope Mom's not in the room. I need time to think. I tell Mike and Tiny Joe to call it a night—and since they look as worn out as I feel, they listen.

"Hello?" I call as I turn the knob, slipping the key card in my pocket.

"Star?"

It's Mom. I can feel my blood pressure climb. I know I have to confront her. I hate confrontations.

She rounds the corner and blinks at me a few times. She's dressed in tight jeans, a white shirt so sheer I can see her bra, and spiky red heels. Her hair is tousled in a professional-looking way. I can't believe it; she's obviously dressed to go somewhere.

"You're going out?" I ask. I can hear my voice climb an octave with anger. Mom looks a little flustered.

"I didn't expect you home so soon, Star," she says, avoiding my glance. I stare at her for a moment.

"Are you serious?" I demand. My hands seem to have clenched into angry fists on their own. "I know you know about the *Dial* interview today. And you were going to go out and keep avoiding me?"

Mom looks temporarily speechless. "Well," she says finally, "I don't know what you want me to say. I thought I'd give you some time to cool down so we could have a rational conversation."

My jaw drops. She looks so smug, I feel like throwing something at her.

"You wanted *me* to cool down?" I ask loudly. "So we could be *rational*? Are you for real? You've kept my father hidden from me for most of my life and you expect that I'm going to be calm about it?"

Mom shrugs dismissively. "You wouldn't understand," she says.

"Try me." My voice is as cold as ice. She stares at me for a moment, then shrugs again.

"Fine," she says with a world-weary sigh, like it's so annoying that I'm asking her to explain. "Your father . . . well, Star, he just wasn't a good father. Or a good husband. He was bad for us, honey. Trust me, this is for your own good."

"I'm supposed to *trust* you? Are you kidding?"

"You're too young to understand," Mom says defensively.

"You are unbelievable," I mutter. I'm getting very, very angry, but I'm trying to keep my temper under control. I need to hear the whole story before I explode. "What about the letters?" I demand. "Is it true that he's been sending them for six years?"

Mom hesitates, and I know she's considering lying.

"Don't, Mom," I say.

"Fine," she says. She sounds almost huffy. Like she has any right to get mad! "Yes. Six years, okay?"

I feel a chill run through me. "My father's been writing me a letter once a month since I was ten, and you didn't tell me?"

"He wasn't a part of our life anymore, Star," she says. "What good could it do?"

"I would have had a chance to have a dad," I say. "I would

have gotten to know my father. I would have realized six years earlier that he still loves me."

"He never loved you," Mom says quickly. "Not the way I do."

"How can you say that?" I can feel tears prickling at the backs of my eyes. I don't even bother blinking them away. "How can you say that when you didn't even love me enough to tell me the truth?"

"It wasn't a matter of love," Mom says sharply. "It was a matter of protecting you from someone who didn't have your best interests at heart."

"You kept me away from my father because you were so intent on making me famous that you didn't want anyone to stop you?" I snap.

"No!" Mom exclaims. "That's not how it is!"

I take in her manicured hands, her new clothes, her expertly tousled hair, her injected face. Everything about her is fake. But at least I always believed that she wanted what was best for me. After all, she's my mom. Isn't that what moms are supposed to do? Love their kids unconditionally and try to do what's best for them?

Instead, she let me down in a way more horrible than I could have imagined.

"I'm done," I say quietly, surprising even myself.

"Done with what?" Mom asks. "Done with yelling at me? So you're finally ready to listen?"

I shake my head slowly.

"No," I say, feeling empty. "I'm done. Done with you. Done with this. Done with all the lies."

Mom laughs, but it sounds hollow.

"Okay, now you're being overdramatic," she says. "This is all you've ever known. You're Star Beck. We're going to put this behind us and move on, just like we always have."

"No," I say. I take a deep breath. "This is different. This is the final straw. I don't even know how often you've lied to me. The Jack and Jill shoe thing? The Melonball soda thing? The nose job? Letting the *Dial* reporter listen in on our lunch without telling me? Those things are all true too, aren't they?"

Mom blanches. "But everything I do is for your own good, sweetheart," she says, not denying any of it. Her voice suddenly sounds pleading, whiny. "You have to understand that."

"I'm done." I take one last look at her. She's staring at me in surprise. I know I've said everything I need to say.

I'm so mad that I can't even stand looking at her anymore.

"Done with what?" she screeches as I walk away. "What are you saying? You can't mean this! Your life is—"

I slam the door to the suite behind me, and her voice, thankfully, disappears. I close my eyes and take a breath. I realize suddenly that I have nowhere to go. The lobby is probably still filled with my fans. I can't go two feet outside the hotel without someone recognizing me. And I'm sure not going back to my mom with my tail between my legs.

Great. That leaves me what? The hallway? I can't pace the hallway forever. Besides, eventually, Mom will come looking for me. And she's the last person in the world I want to see.

I stand there for a moment, feeling completely displaced. I bang my head against the wall in frustration a few times. Then, with my forehead aching, I suddenly realize where I'll go.

"Well, come in, kiddo," Ben says, holding his hotel room door open for me. "I was just about to go work out." He's wearing a faded gray Beatles T-shirt with a hole just under his right armpit and a pair of black workout pants with a white stripe down each side.

"Oh," I say, and hesitate in the doorway. "I don't want to interrupt you."

"I hate working out anyhow," he says with a shrug. "Lifting weights is boring. And I actually fell off the treadmill last week because I was so busy watching *The Office* that I didn't notice when the speed changed."

I laugh even though I'm miserable.

"So actually," he concludes, "you're pretty much saving me from myself. What's up, Star? You okay? Come on in."

I follow Ben inside. The two beds and the chair are covered with clothes and shoes and guitar strings and general Ben stuff.

Ben swipes a giant pile of clothes off the edge of each bed. "Have a seat."

I sit down on the corner of one of his double beds. He sits down on the other bed.

"What'd she do this time?" he asks finally.

"What *didn't* she do?" I mutter.

"Start from the beginning," Ben says. And so I do. Not the *beginning* beginning, because not only does Ben already know it all, but it would take about two years to go through all the problems Mom and I have. But at the beginning of today. The "mother-daughter day." The magazine reporter. My fight with Mom.

Her admission about my long-lost dad.

By the time I'm done, Ben is just staring at me.

"I can't believe it," he says finally. "I mean, I knew she was cold. But she was keeping your dad from you? For six years?"

I nod. I don't know what else to say.

"Star, that's horrible."

"I know."

"How'd you turn out so normal?" Ben asks after a moment.

It's something I've often wondered myself. But heaven forbid I say it out loud to Mom. After all, *normal* is a bad word in her vocabulary. Sometimes I wonder how I could possibly even be related to her. "It's not like she spends any time with me anyhow," I finally say. "I might as well have raised myself."

"You pretty much did," Ben mutters. After a moment, he puts a hand on my knee and looks me in the eye. "So what are you going to do?"

"I have to go find him," I say, trying to sound braver than I feel. I *know* it's what I have to do. I just don't know how. Ben looks surprised.

"Your dad?"

"Don't I have to?" I ask. "At least let him know that I wasn't getting the letters? That I wish I could have known him during the last six years? Maybe he's normal. Maybe I have one parent who actually loves me—not my money—after all."

"But what if he's not the dad you hope he is?" Ben asks slowly. "What if he's just like your mom?"

"He couldn't be," I say, shaking my head. "No way. And anyhow, it's not just about him. Ben, I can't stay here. I'm so sick of everything. I feel like everyone's using me and lying to me. I don't know who to trust anymore."

"You can trust me," Ben says.

"I know," I say. I hesitate. "I just have to get out of here for a little while. I need to be someplace where every camera isn't always on me, where I can walk outside without getting mobbed, where I can have a bad hair day or be in a bad mood or have a pimple without it being blogged about and making national news."

The plan is crystallizing in my head as I hear myself say the words.

"But you're Star Beck." Ben states the obvious. "Everywhere you go, people will recognize you."

"Unless I don't look like me," I say, gathering steam. "Unless I look and act totally different."

"How are you going to do that?" Ben asks skeptically. He eyes my long red curls. "You're kind of distinctive-looking."

I already have an answer. "I could change my look. I could change my name. After all, I'm an actress, aren't I? I could act differently, talk differently."

"I don't know . . . ," Ben says skeptically. He studies me for a minute. "It might work if people didn't know you were missing. But as soon as word gets out that *Star Beck* has run away or whatever, someone will recognize you for sure."

"Do you really think my mother would tell the media that I'm gone?" I ask, arching an eyebrow at him. A look of realization crosses his face as I continue. "No," I answer my own question wearily. "Because then she'd have to admit that we got into a fight, and she wants the world to see her as the perfect mother." I shake my head at the irony of it all. "She'll cover for me just to save face. So no one—except maybe a few people Mom hires—will even know they're supposed to be looking for me."

I'll have to go now. Tonight. It will be much easier to disappear from a hotel than from our compound back in L.A. And Mom is so shaken up over our conversation that she won't have considered yet that I might have run away.

Ben nods slowly. "But how long do you think you can pull it off?"

"Just long enough for me to catch my breath," I say, trying to imagine a day with no paparazzi. "And hopefully long enough for me to find my dad."

"I don't know, Star. It sounds kinda crazy." Ben looks me in the eye. "Are you sure about this?"

"More than I've ever been about anything else in my life," I say. And I am.

I wanna step back,
Impact,
Change my world.
I wanna do it all,
See it all,
I'm not a little girl.

—"IF I FALL," STAR BECK
ALBUM: *THIS LIFE*

★

Chapter 6

What does it take to change your look? Not as much as you'd think. I once had to dress up as both an "evil" and a "good" version of myself on *Secrets of My Teenage Life*. My stylist and I had a blast. When I had looked in the mirror at a blond, pigtailed "good" girl in a Catholic-school uniform and a halo, I barely recognized myself. I was even less recognizable in my dark-haired "evil" version, dressed in black from head to toe and covered in goth makeup.

The lesson I learned? Take away the trademark red curls, change my makeup and my clothes . . . and it's not so hard to reinvent myself.

Assuming that my mom has gone out for the evening, since she was all dressed up, I send Ben to knock on the door.

"The coast is clear," he reports a few minutes later. I follow him back up and we walk quietly inside. All that remains of my mother is the heavy scent of Chanel No. 5 hanging in the air. Still, I don't know how soon she'll be back. I have to move quickly.

I walk into the bathroom and look in the mirror. I lift up a handful of my red hair, knowing it's the first thing, the main thing, that has to go.

"Hasta la vista," I murmur.

I find some tiny scissors Melissa uses to cut dangling threads off my clothing. They'll have to do. It's not like I can just go find Don and ask for a makeover. I take a deep breath. Then I start snipping.

Handful upon handful of thick red hair drops to the carpet, and in less than five minutes, my waist-length curls have been shortened to a sloppy, choppy, chin-length bob. I look in the mirror and wince. It's *horrible.* Clearly, I have no future in hairdressing. But this isn't about looking good.

I whisper a silent apology to the hotel and the plumbers who will be called in later as I flush my hair down the toilet until it has all disappeared.

"You okay in there?" Ben calls from the other room, where he's nervously standing guard.

"I'm fine!" I yell back, wishing that I really meant it.

Next, I grab a package of my mother's hair dye and regard it warily. She carries a kit with her just in case her roots begin to show before she can get to a decent salon (as if that would be the worst thing in the world). The directions say something about foil wraps and combing on the blond color only where you want it, but I don't have time for that. Besides, my chopped-up hair is pretty much a lost cause. No point in attempting to look attractive now. I wet my hair in the sink, open the bottle, squeeze the strong-smelling cream into my palm and work it quickly into my hair. I run to the other room, where I grab a big tote bag and pack a few changes of T-shirts, underwear, bras and an extra pair of jeans. I throw some sneakers and socks in too, as well as flip-flops and a pair of pajamas. I pack a small bag of makeup, then my toothbrush and toothpaste. Finally, not feeling particularly bad about it, since I'm the one who earned it, I lift up the clothing in Mom's large suitcase to reveal the secret zippered compartment below. I know she keeps cash in there. I stuff roughly a thousand dollars in twenties and fifties into the zippered inner

compartment of my tote bag, then unzip her smaller suitcase, which sits in the corner, and take all the cash in its
hidden compartment too. Seven hundred-dollar bills, three
twenties, a ten and six ones. I stuff those in my pocket. It
should be enough to get me where I need to go.

I'm going to Florida. To find my dad. It doesn't feel real
to me.

I take my cell out of my bag and leave it on the counter,
like any good *Law & Order* fan. I know the police can track
your phone, even if you don't use it, just by tracking down
which cell towers it pings off of.

I go back to the bathroom and wash the highlighter out of
my hair. Then I pull the hair dryer from the wall, set it to
high and bend over. I'm done in just a few minutes, thanks
to the new length. As I stand to regard myself in the mirror,
I burst out laughing. My hair is an unnatural shade of
blondish red. I look like a cross between Bozo the Clown and
Little Orphan Annie. If the paparazzi could see me now ...

I change out of my wet shirt into a nondescript I LOVE NEW
YORK tee I got the last time we were in Manhattan. I rifle
through my bag until I find the gray Dodgers cap I wore
home from my show tonight. I put it on over my crazily colored hair. I remove my contact lenses, which I almost always wear, and replace them with the red-rimmed glasses
I sometimes wear to read in bed. I check myself in the

mirror one more time. Unattractive and unrecognizable. Just the way I want it.

"Wow," Ben says, staring at me as I emerge into the hallway.

"I know," I say. "Good-bye, Star Beck. Hello . . . weird-haired, glasses-wearing, normal girl."

Ben smiles, but he doesn't look happy.

"I hope this is the right thing, Star," he says. "Is this what you really want?"

"Yes," I say without hesitating. It *is*. "I know it seems like I've made a snap decision. But I have to get away from all this. I have to find my dad. It's crazy, but it feels right."

"I just . . . I'm thinking now that maybe I shouldn't have been so gung-ho about helping you," Ben says. "I forget sometimes that you're only sixteen. I mean, this is illegal."

"It's fine," I say firmly.

"But—"

"I'm fine," I repeat with false confidence. "No one will ever know you helped. I promise. And Ben, honestly, I would have done this with or without you."

He looks at me for a moment, as if trying to decide something. Then he nods.

"Listen. I think the best thing for you to do is travel south by bus," he says. "They'll ask for ID, but you can talk them into letting you on without one, I think."

"Okay." How different can a public bus be from my tour bus? Yeah. I decide not to think that way.

"Other than that, I don't know how else I can help you," he says. "You can't call me. Once they discover you're missing, they'll put a trace on my phone. Your mom knows we're friends. If you need me, make sure to call from a landline and end the call quickly."

"I watch *CSI* too," I say, rolling my eyes.

"That you do," he says. He reaches out and pulls me into a hug. "I believe in you, Star."

"Thanks," I say. I wonder why Ben seems to be the only one in my world who really does.

When I arrive on the first floor a few moments later, I spot a man, a woman and two teenage girls exiting the elevator next to mine. I fall into step behind them, hoping that anyone on the lookout for Star Beck will just assume I'm a random teenager who belongs to this family.

As I stroll behind my new family out of the Regency's lobby a few minutes later, I pass a small cluster of my fans, who are perched sleepily on armchairs with I LOVE YOU, STAR! signs propped up on their laps, apparently waiting to catch a glimpse of me. I even hear one of them muttering that

I'm too high maintenance to come down and see my fans. Whatever. I hold my breath and try to slow my pounding heart as I saunter casually by. A few of them glance my way, but unbelievably, no one seems to know me. I feel strangely free as I step outside, fall back from my new "family" as they turn down the street and wait for the Regency's valet to hail me a cab.

As I ask the driver to take me to the bus station, I realize I've passed my first test. I exhale loudly. I've slipped out of my own hotel, past a handful of my devoted fans, and no one realized it was me.

My nervous energy gives way to a nagging question in the pit of my stomach. Is Ben right? Am I doing the right thing? I don't know. In less than an hour, I've made a decision to walk away from the only life I've ever known. Maybe it's the stupidest thing I've ever done.

Either way, I'm free. For once in my life, I'm not Star Beck. Until this moment, I never fully realized how much I was dying to be someone—*anyone*—other than me.

Let it go (oh, oh, oh),
I'm moving on;
Yesterday is so yesterday—
I'm walking into tomorrow.

—"IF I FALL," STAR BECK
ALBUM: *THIS LIFE*

★

Chapter 7

One of the lights is flickering eerily outside Port Authority as I hoist my tote bag over my shoulder and head inside. I gulp, blink and try to steel myself. *This is the right thing to be doing.* It has to be. I try to ignore the pang of guilt inside me as I think about how worried everyone will be when they realize I'm gone.

My hat pulled low over my face and my glasses still

perched on my nose, I follow the signs to the bus counter. I approach the window, where an agent is flipping through a magazine. She looks up lazily as I approach.

"Can I help you?" she asks in a thick accent I can't quite identify. I take a deep breath.

"I need a ticket to Florida," I say. "St. Petersburg."

She stares at me for a moment.

"Hon," she says, peering at me closely. I don't think I'm imagining the suspicion in her eyes as she looks at me. "It's the middle of the night. There ain't no tickets to Florida 'til morning. Besides, you got to get a bus to Tampa. It's the closest stop we got. Don't no buses go direct to St. Pete. First Tampa bus is at seven a.m., but it's already sold out. Next bus ain't till noon."

I may have planned this poorly. The longer I stay here, the greater the chance I'll get caught. Even though I've disguised myself, it's not like I've brought along an invisibility cloak. Someone is sure to recognize me if they realize they're supposed to be looking. I need to get out of New York as soon as possible.

"Is there, um, *any* bus leaving tonight?" I ask nervously.

"One," she says. "The early-morning to Charlotte, North Carolina. Leaves in fifteen minutes, though. You want in? It gets in at seven-ten p.m. tomorrow. You can catch a direct bus to Tampa from there."

"Yes, yes, please," I say hurriedly. I hand her two fifties

and a ten for the $101 fare, and she hands me a bus ticket and my change.

It isn't until I'm putting my change back in my wallet and the agent has returned to her reading that I notice she's flipping through last month's *Glamour* magazine. The one with *me* on the cover.

A warm glow spreads through me as I realize she hasn't had even a flash of recognition, hasn't batted an eyelash at this strange, orangey-blond-haired girl in front of her, even though her nose is now buried in a magazine full of pictures of Star Beck.

For the first time, I realize that it's very possible I can get away with this after all.

The bus is dark and dingy. As we pull away from the station, I slouch down in my seat and try to stop my heart from pounding so hard. I turn and watch as the brightly lit buildings of New York's skyline, punctuated by the Empire State Building and the Chrysler Building, disappear behind us.

As the bus rolls on, heading south, no one else on board even glances at me. For once in my life, I'm anonymous. No paparazzi. No fans. No stares or whispers. I've done it. I've escaped. No one has followed me. No one knows. No one is looking at me, wondering if I'm Star Beck. I'm just a girl in a ball cap with weird hair, headed to Charlotte.

Who knew it would be so easy to disappear, identityless, into the night?

And finally, as the vibrations of the bus course through me and the other passengers gradually sink into silence, I fall into a troubled sleep.

I don't open my eyes until almost noon the next day. The landscape has changed. Gone are the rows of suburban homes and neighborhoods set in nestling hills. We're passing through expansive fields now, with hundreds of workers dressed in tattered clothes picking things off plants as we whiz by.

I sit up a bit straighter and yawn. My whole body feels stiff. I lean into the bus window as I gaze outside, and the glass feels cool against my forehead.

I wonder what my mom is doing right now. Is she panicked, looking for me, wringing her hands and wondering if something awful has happened to me? Or did she simply shrug off the search an hour after I disappeared, change into her La Perla nightgown, take a sleeping pill and crawl into her feather bed with a lazy yawn, her cheetah mask covering her eyes?

I can almost see her drying her tears and saying, "Yes, it's quite a shame she's gone. But I'm sure she'll turn up. Now if you'll excuse me, I must get my beauty sleep." I can even hear the heavy sigh she would heave for dramatic effect.

Still, I feel guilty.

Because as bad as the things are that she's done to me, isn't running away without so much as leaving a note even worse?

As the bus rumbles on into the southern afternoon, I try not to think about it. Instead, I think of the future and what will happen when I see my dad again. What it will be like to live a normal life—even if it's only for a few days.

"End of the line!" the driver announces over the intercom as we finally draw to a halt in a bus station in Charlotte, the brakes squeaking in protest. "Everybody off!"

I stand up, along with the rest of the sleepy-looking passengers, and file off the bus, hoisting my tote bag over my shoulder and trying to blend in, hoping that no one notices me now in the thinning twilight. Outside the bus, the air is humid and sticky, a distinct difference from the crisp autumn chill of New York.

I get in line for the only ticket window that's open.

"I need a ticket to Tampa, Florida, please," I say once it's my turn.

"Next bus to Tampa doesn't leave for three hours," says the ticket lady without even looking up. "You want a ticket?"

"Oh. I guess so," I say, feeling my heart sink a bit. I'll be basically a sitting duck just lounging in a bus terminal for three hours. Someone is bound to recognize me eventually. Maybe I'll walk outside the station while I wait and see if I can find a place to eat. Now that we've stopped, I'm realizing that my stomach is growling at me.

I pay for my trip to Tampa. I feel a strange sense of comfort as the agent presses the paper ticket into my hand. This is it. I'm finally officially on my way to find my dad.

On my way out of the station, I pass several uniformed police officers, who are glancing around at the crowd. I duck my head, just in case they're looking for me, but none of them gives me a second glance. Clearly, I'm being paranoid.

I walk across the street to the first restaurant I see, a place called Mel's Diner, careful to keep my hat pulled low.

I slink into a corner booth and sit down, breathing in the strangely comforting smells of fried food and freshly brewed coffee.

The diner is only half full, and the odds that anyone in here would recognize me are slim. There are four construction workers at one of the tables. One of them is still wearing his hard hat. At another table, a pleasant-looking couple peer at the menu through their bifocals. There's a tired-looking mother at another table tending to two toddlers and a screaming infant in a stroller. And at the counter, there are a couple of middle-aged men. I relax a bit. Definitely not the typical Star Beck audience, thank goodness.

"You alone today, hon?" asks the plump, middle-aged waitress who approaches my table after I've been sitting there for a moment, gazing around. She has glasses hanging from a multicolored string around her neck and gray hair pulled back into a wispy pony tail.

"Yes, I am," I say, looking up a bit so as not to be rude but still being careful to keep my face concealed under the hat.

"Sorry, hon," she says apologetically, "but singles have to sit at the counter. We keep the booths for groups. It'll start getting crowded in here in about thirty minutes when the eight o'clock buses come in."

"Oh," I say, my heart starting to race. In the corner booth, I can hunch down and escape being noticed. But can I do that at the counter, surrounded by people? The men at the counter are chatting with one another, sipping coffee, flipping through newspapers and watching the two TVs mounted overhead.

The waitress pats me on the back as I stand up.

"Sorry, hon," she says again, leading me to an empty stool and placing a laminated menu in front of me. "I'll buy you a Coke to make it up to you. Okay?"

I force a nervous smile. "Thanks." But my nerves are on full alert now. What if someone recognizes me?

I pick up the menu, scanning its offerings. Suddenly it occurs to me: for the first time in years, I can have whatever I want for dinner. I think back to the French restaurant in New York. I haven't had a hamburger since I was twelve. I can hardly remember what they taste like. And fries? I'm allowed the occasional half baked potato, but I would give my left arm for a pile of greasy French fries.

Thankfully, no one wants my left arm today. They just want $6.99 for a burger and fries. I order quickly and ask for a chocolate milk shake too. I might as well go all out. I'm practically salivating thinking about it.

"You okay, hon?" the waitress asks after I've placed my order. My heart starts thudding again. Why is she asking me that?

"I'm fine," I choke out nervously, hoping to avoid any more of this conversation. I need to focus on looking less jittery. I take a couple of deep breaths and focus on the TV in the corner, just in case the waitress has any ideas about striking up another conversation with me. I pretend that I'm thoroughly absorbed in what the CNN anchors are saying to each other, although I'm barely paying attention.

Until I hear my own name.

"And now for our entertainment report," says the anchor with a smile, turning to a dark-haired woman beside her. "Adriana, you're going to tell us tonight about pop star Star Beck?"

The people around me at the counter are looking at the TV too, and I feel suddenly nauseous. For a moment, I'm sure that they're going to announce that I'm missing and everyone should keep an eye out for me. I squeeze my eyes closed and wait for the inevitable. But then the entertainment reporter begins to speak.

"We haven't confirmed this independently yet, but there's word from sources inside Star Beck's camp that the teen pop star was admitted to rehab this morning," says the reporter.

What? Rehab? My eyes pop open. Rehab from what?

"Rehab?" asks the anchor, echoing my thoughts. "But she's only sixteen."

"Well," continues the reporter enthusiastically, "it's just a rumor at this point. But she hasn't been seen since last night. Her mother, Laura Beck, and her publicist are saying

she's just under the weather. But an intern at her management company has given interviews to a few New York
stations saying that she's actually been taken away to
Lovesdale, an ultraprivate rehab center in upstate New
York that specializes in alcohol addiction."

"Alcohol addiction?" the anchor presses. I stare at the TV
screen.

"It's a sad fact with young stars today," the reporter continues. "They start drinking practically as soon as they can
walk. And this isn't the first time these rumors have
dogged Star Beck."

Yeah, no kidding. When I was hospitalized last summer
for heatstroke after an outdoor show in ninety-five-degree
heat, all the celebrity magazines said it was alcohol poi-
soning and that I had to have my stomach pumped. When
I sprained my ankle in August and had to miss a sched-
uled appearance on *The Tonight Show*, a rumor started
that I had fallen in a nightclub because I'd had too much
to drink. I hadn't even *been* at the nightclub, never mind
the fact that I don't drink. Are you kidding? Do you really
think the mom who doesn't let me have ranch dressing
with my celery sticks is going to let me walk around chug-
ging vodka?

"It's a shame," the anchor is saying on TV, shaking her
head. "Star Beck seems so sweet."

"Well, it's the sweet ones you have to worry about," the

75

entertainment reporter chuckles. "Besides, if she's not in rehab, why hasn't her publicist had her come forward to address these allegations today?"

At least the media doesn't realize I've run away. But now the whole world thinks I'm such an alcoholic that I'm doing a stint in rehab at age sixteen.

Typical.

"Good point indeed. Thanks, Adriana," says the anchor. "We'll be back after the break." As they fade to commercial, they play the video for my song "Waiting." I watch my own face on the screen until it switches to a commercial for some headache medicine. It's only then that I start breathing again.

I look around nervously, sure that at least one of the patrons around me will be sneaking suspicious looks at me. *Hey, aren't you the alcoholic who's supposed to be in rehab?* But they're chatting with each other, flipping through their papers, eating their meals, just like they were before the CNN report came on. It doesn't seem to have occurred to anyone that the pop star who's supposed to be in rehab is actually sitting down the counter from them at a diner in Charlotte. Then again, why would it?

Just then, the waitress appears with a steaming basket filled with fries and a burger that would have looked perfect to me ten minutes earlier. But now, my stomach is so tied in knots that I can't even handle looking at the food, which should smell delicious. Instead, it just makes my stomach turn.

"Thanks," I say. I flash her the brightest smile I can handle. "Would you mind telling me where the bathroom is?"

I splash some cool water on my face, then lock myself in one of the stalls. I lean my head against the cool metal door, close my eyes and rack my brain.

Call me stupid, but somehow, I hadn't expected to see my own face on CNN less than twenty-four hours after I ran away. Obviously Mom and Mariska are trying to keep my disappearance under wraps, so it's not like the world is going to be out looking for me. But the story has put me on the public's radar, even if the world thinks I'm locked away at Lovesdale.

"I can't get back on a bus," I mumble, not caring that it's probably not normal to be talking to myself in the bathroom. "What if someone sees me?"

It dawns on me that I'm really lucky to have made it even this far. Sure, I look totally different. I hardly recognize myself when I look at my short, orange-blond hair and glasses in the mirror. But all it would take is one die-hard fan who happens to be riding the Charlotte-to-Tampa route. My heart sinks. What am I going to do? I can't stay locked in a diner bathroom for the rest of my life.

I pound my head against the cool metal of the stall door again. Suddenly, a sliver of white catches my eye. I blink a few times, lean back from the door and stare at the piece of paper taped to the metal, inches away from where I was self-destructively banging.

USED CAR FOR SALE: CASH ONLY. $1000 OUT THE DOOR, it says. I gulp and lean forward to read the fine print. *1968 VW Beetle convertible in good condition, 178,000 miles. Must sell. Ask at the counter.*

Okay. Now, I don't usually believe in signs. But come on, can it be pure coincidence that there's a car for sale mere inches from where I was halfheartedly trying to put myself into a coma moments earlier?

I think no.

"I'll buy a car," I say aloud, still not all that concerned that I have apparently begun having whole conversations with myself in the bathroom. "I'll buy a car," I repeat more firmly. "I'll drive to Florida."

After all, I have a driver's license. Most of the time, I get chauffeured around, of course. But Mariska thought it would be a cool idea to do the driver's test with a reporter and video guy from *Access Hollywood* in the backseat to prove that I'm just a normal teen (as if normal teenagers take Billy Bush and a video camera along on their driving tests). I actually passed on my first try (although maybe not every DMV guy straightens the cones out for test takers. But regardless, I *did* learn how to drive—on my mom's manual transmission vintage Porsche, which, believe me, was not easy).

With a new sense of resolve flooding through me, I glance once more at the car flyer, leave the stall, smooth my new bangs over the slight bump I've given myself on my forehead and walk calmly out of the bathroom.

I manage to eat half of my burger before the waitress comes over to check on me. "Um, I saw the sign for the car for sale in the bathroom," I say.

The waitress nods. "Yep," she says noncommittally. "Why, you interested?"

"Yeah," I say. "Do you know who I can talk to?"

"That would be me," she says. "But come on. You got a thousand dollars on you? You're just a kid."

"I have a thousand dollars," I say right away, without even thinking about the fact that that's probably not the best thing to go around admitting to people.

"Really," the waitress says flatly, arching an eyebrow and looking at me like she doesn't really believe me.

"Well . . . yeah," I say. Suddenly I feel nervous. I notice that the guy two seats down from me at the bar has taken an interest in our conversation.

"Maple, you tryin' to con this girl outta her money?" the guy asks. He smiles at me.

"Teddy, you stay outta this," Maple replies. Teddy, who looks like he's old enough to be my grandfather, rolls his eyes.

"That car ain't worth a cent more than eight hundred," he says, loudly enough that I know he means for Maple to hear. She rolls her eyes back at him.

"That's not true," she says. "It's worth a thousand. Just like it says on the flyer."

"Aw, come on, Maple," Teddy says. "Give the kid a break. How about eight-fifty?"

"Nine-fifty," Maple retorts.

"Nine hundred," Teddy says. "And that's our final offer."

Maple looks at the two of us for a minute before sighing.

"Fine," she says. She looks back at me. "Now you wanna see the car, or what?"

She storms off without another word. I turn to Teddy.

"Um, thanks," I say, mystified. He shrugs.

"Don't mention it," he says with a grin. "I love arguin' with that woman. Makes my day. But if you want to use some of that extra hundred to pay for my dinner . . ."

I dig out a twenty and lay it on the counter, figuring it'll cover both of us.

"Thank you kindly," Teddy says. "Now you gonna follow Maple and get that car?"

I quickly pick up my bag and scurry after Maple, who has disappeared out the back door.

Maple's standing beside the Beetle, which to my surprise is painted bright pink. I hadn't noticed that in the black-and-white ad in the bathroom.

"I was a bit of a girly girl in the seventies," Maple admits with a sheepish grin when she sees my reaction. "I don't have much use for a bright pink Beetle now. But it runs great. My ex-husband was a mechanic, and he kept it up real good."

I expected something old and beat-up, but it actually doesn't look bad. I don't see any dents, and even though it isn't new and shiny or anything, the pink paint still looks decent, and when Maple turns it on for me, it sounds like it runs pretty well. Not that I know much about cars.

"I'm a fool for letting this go for under a thousand," Maple mutters as she gets out and I slide into the driver's seat. "This was my first car."

"It's nice," I say softly as I move the seat forward and put my hands on the wheel. Maple shrugs.

"I finally decided I don't need it anymore," she says. "So you're doing me a favor anyways. All the dealership would offer was five hundred dollars. Highway robbery, I tell you." She shakes her head when I go to touch the radio dial. "Doesn't work."

"It's perfect," I insist.

"Well, that'll be nine hundred bucks, kiddo," she says. I reach into my pocket and hand her the money.

She hands me the title and tells me that I need to fill out the back of it with my name and address, the date of sale and the odometer reading. I fudge on the details, scribbling a nearly illegible *Amanda Beckendale* and a fake address instead of my own. Maple yells inside for Teddy (who, along with being a pro car haggler, also happens to be a notary, I learn). He comes out back to sign and stamp the title, grumbling the whole time that his meat loaf is getting cold. Then Maple signs the back of the title herself and gives me directions to the motor vehicle bureau on nearby Brookshire Boulevard.

"You just have to drop the title off there, and they'll transfer the car and the tags to your name," she says. I nod, knowing that I can't actually do that. What if they ask for my license? I have the feeling I was darned lucky that Teddy was more worried about his waiting meat loaf than he was about asking me for ID. I doubt I'd be so lucky at the motor vehicle bureau. But I promise Maple I'll take care of the plates and the paperwork. And I will—someday.

"Take good care of my car, girl," Maple says. She bends

down, kisses the pink hood and gives it one last pat. She looks up at me. "And take care of yourself too."

"I will," I promise.

I restart the car, wave to Maple and slowly pull out of the parking lot in my new pink Beetle, feeling freer than I've ever felt in my life.

Home is where the heart is,
Or so they say,
But my heart's with you,
baby (hey, hey).
I'm coming home,
I'm coming home.
But will you leave me
(oh, oh, oh),
Will you leave me the key?

—"WHERE THE HEART," STAR BECK
ALBUM: *STAR LIGHT*

★

Chapter 8

The drive to Florida is long and boring, and it doesn't help that night has now fallen and I'm speeding south through the darkness, but I'm buoyed by the thoughts of freedom—and a new life.

The difficulty of driving a manual car keeps me awake. I forgot how tough it is to shift gears using the clutch. I even stall at an intersection before I get out of North Carolina. Thankfully, there's no one behind me at the time.

With each milestone I hit—the South Carolina border, Savannah, Jacksonville—my heart pounds just a bit faster. I find an old map in the glove compartment and I take I-10 West from Jacksonville to I-75 South. This will branch into I-275 and take me into St. Petersburg, where my dad lives.

I stop for gas and a handful of road maps at five a.m. in Gainesville; then I stop at McDonald's because I'm starving and no one can tell me I can't. Plus, I need desperately to use the bathroom. I take a bite of my Sausage McMuffin in the parking lot, and my eyes widen. It's so good. I've never had a McMuffin in my life. Sure, I know they're probably terrible for me, that I'd probably burst right out of my stupid gold hot pants after just one, but my macrobiotic meals and small slices of fruit don't hold a candle to the McMuff.

As I hit Wildwood, just an hour north of Tampa, I'm bouncing in my seat like the toddler I was the last time I saw my father. I start humming, because that's what I always do when I'm nervous. It's a musician thing, I think.

I know I'm driving south into a new beginning, a new chance, as a new person, with a father I haven't known since I was a young kid. I know that for a little while, at least, I've left my pop star world behind. I know that for at least a bit, I can just be *me*.

But I wonder if I even know who that is anymore. Maybe I've been too busy being Star Beck the pop star to remember how to just be Amanda Beckendale, sixteen-year-old girl.

By the time I cross the long Howard Frankland Bridge to St. Petersburg, I'm exhausted. I decide to find a place to stay before I go meet my father. I need some time to gather my thoughts and figure out what I'll say when I find him.

I get off at the first exit, passing a shopping center, a grocery store and a Bennigan's. I pass another few restaurants and stores; then I notice the peeling Star Light Motel sign flickering a block farther down the road. I laugh out loud at the name. It's practically calling to me. The place doesn't look remotely like the five-star hotels I'm used to. But how bad can it be? Besides, with my name flickering at me in big red letters, how can I say no?

I turn right into its parking lot, and ten minutes later, I have my answer. After finding out from the drunk-looking clerk that a single room there is just $29 a night, or $189 if I want to pay by the week, I decide to pay for a week up front, because I have the feeling it may take me a few days to work up the courage to get back into my dad's life. As I congratulate myself on getting what sounds like such a good deal, he hands me a rusty key and points outside, toward the back of the building. "Room one-twelve. You can pull your car right up in front."

I thank him and repark the Beetle in front of the door to room 112. I get out and try the key in the lock. It takes a few minutes of jiggling, but finally, the door opens into a dingy, dimly lit room. I flip on the light.

It's quite possibly the worst place I've ever seen. The green carpet looks like stale pea soup, and it's so worn in places that I can see patches of the bare floor underneath. There's a wooden bureau that's cracked and chipped and missing one of its six drawers. The double bed is covered with a threadbare orange comforter that looks like it came from the 1970s, and it's sagging in the middle. The bathroom door is open wide enough for me to see the flickering fluorescent light, the stained tiles and the rusty handle of an ancient-looking toilet.

"It's not so bad," I say to myself, trying to sound cheerful. "You can stay here for a week, anyhow. By then, you'll have found your dad. You'll be fine. Stop being such a wimp." I've almost convinced myself that I'll be okay when I spot a huge cockroach skittering across a bare spot in the carpet and disappearing under the bed.

I scream and slam the door to the room.

No. No, no, no. I cannot stay here. I cannot stay in a dingy motel room that looks like it hasn't been cleaned since before I was born. I can't share a dingy motel room with a *cockroach*.

I hurry back to the front of the building and toss the key across the desk at the dozing clerk.

"Huh?" His eyes snap open as he hears the key ping off the desk.

"I can't stay here," I say.

"Why not?" he asks, narrowing his eyes at me. I realize I'm shaking. I can't stop seeing the giant cockroach in my mind.

"It's . . . it's just awful!" I exclaim. His eyes narrow even further, and I feel compelled to explain. "I mean, no offense," I say quickly, remembering my manners. "But it's dirty. And the dresser is broken. And the carpet is all worn. And there's a *cockroach*!" I exclaim, expecting him to gasp in disgust. Instead, he just laughs.

"Just one?" he chortles. "Dream on!" My stomach turns.

"That's gross," I say bluntly.

He shrugs.

"I don't see the problem," he mumbles.

I stare at him, incredulous. "There are *cockroaches* in my

room," I repeat slowly. "And the place is disgusting. Didn't you hear me?"

I pause and take a deep breath, worried that I'm being a diva. I hate being a diva.

"So don't stay there," the clerk says with a shrug and a smirk. I sigh. I feel like I'm talking to a wall.

"That's my point," I say. "I can't. I won't stay here. Can I have my money back now, please?"

The clerk laughs and taps a plastic sign propped up on the desk. My eyes slowly glide over to it, and my heart sinks. ABSOLUTELY NO REFUNDS, it says.

"But I didn't know!" I exclaim. "Can't you make an exception?"

He taps the signs again, still smirking at me. I squint and realize that in small print below the NO REFUNDS line is another line. NO EXCEPTIONS, it says. I groan.

"Oh, come on! Please?" I beg. I can't afford to lose two hundred dollars and to have to shell out at least that much for another hotel. For once, I can't plunk down my American Express Centurion card to make everything all right.

On top of that, I suspect it isn't exactly legal for sixteen-year-olds to go around booking hotel rooms on their own.

"No exceptions," the clerk says, tapping the sign insistently.

"But—" I start to protest. He laughs and cuts me off.

"What did you expect for a hundred and eighty-nine dollars a week?" he asks, arching an eyebrow at me.

I open my mouth to answer, then snap it shut again, because I don't know what to say. Honestly, I have no idea what I expected. It's not like I've ever had to pay for a room before.

"I don't know," I admit. "What do hotels usually cost?"

"The Best Western down the street?" he says. "They charge you ninety-nine dollars a night. The Days Inn on Thirty-fourth Street? They're seventy-five dollars a night. And the Hilton downtown? Well, they start at one sixty-nine."

"A night?" I ask incredulously. I do the mental math. I'd be out on the street in less than three days.

"A night," he confirms triumphantly. "Sure makes the beautiful Star Light Motel sound like a deal, don't it?"

"Yeah, I guess it does," I finally mumble, discouraged. I can't even afford the Best Western. I'd run out of money in just a few days. I hardly have enough money to eat as it is.

"So I expect you'll be wanting this back now?" he asks, holding up the key. I sigh. He grins, tossing the key back across the desk to me. I stare at it for a moment.

"Welcome home," says the clerk, suddenly perking up, "to the Star Light Motel."

After chasing the giant cockroach for fifteen minutes and trying to kill him with my shoe, I finally manage to get him to run out the front door and then spend the *next* fifteen minutes checking behind the dusty blinds, under the bed and in the bathroom for any other sign of life. I try—mostly unsuccessfully—to forget about the fact that he probably has a whole family hiding in the walls. I nap for about two hours, thanks to my overwhelming exhaustion and the fact that I've just driven nine hours straight to get here. I lie perfectly still, sure that at any moment, one of the horrible little bugs will climb across me and I'll completely lose it.

Thankfully, that doesn't happen. It seems the roaches prefer sticking to the floor.

Nine a.m. I need to buy some Raid. I've seen the commercials where Suzy Housewife points a can of Raid at an unsuspecting animated roach, and he turns around like he's in a stickup, puts his spindly little arms in the air . . . and keels over, dead.

Sounds pretty good to me.

I try the bedside radio alarm clock, twisting the dial a few times until I pick up a station that comes in clearly. I laugh out loud as a song materializes through the static.

It's "You're the One," the song I generally lead my concerts off with.

"You've got to be kidding me." I listen to the song, absently humming along with the tinny radio, until it ends.

"Today, we're talking about Star Beck," says a deejay's solemn, deep voice when the song ends. "Is she in rehab? Her mother and her publicist claim she's sick and is confined to her hotel room, but an intern for her record label has said she's been checked into a rehab center for alcohol addiction. What do you think? We're taking your calls all morning. The number to call is 1-888-55-MAGIC. Sound off on the air about what's really happened to Star Beck."

There's a pause, and I turn the radio up, listening intently.

"Go ahead, caller. You're on the air," says the deejay.

There's a moment of heavy breathing on the other end; then a girl's voice says. "Yes. I'm just really scared for her, that's all. She's my favorite singer. She's so cool. I don't know why she'd be an alcoholic. She's probably just sick, you know?"

"Opinions seem to be divided," the deejay says. There are a few seconds of silence.

"Plus," the girl adds, "it would be wrong if she drank that much, you know?"

The deejay laughs. "Seems Star Beck isn't setting a great example for her young fans. Then again, celebrities never do, do they?"

I feel terrible as the deejay takes his next call. I haven't even thought about the message I'll be sending to my fans by disappearing. I've only been focused on getting away from all the insanity and on finding my dad.

"Hello, caller, you're on the air," says the deejay, breaking into my thoughts.

"Hi," says a male voice. "I'm Josh calling from St. Pete Beach and I just want to say that I'm worried about Star Beck," he says. "Alcohol addiction is a serious thing."

"Indeed it is," the deejay says gravely. I feel even worse.

"My church group prayed for her last night," Josh says.

The deejay chuckles. "Well, Josh, I'm sure that'll help.

"And now, folks, it's time for a commercial break."

I didn't realize that I'd be painted in the media as an alcoholic, of all things, if I vanished. I didn't consider all the people who would be worrying about me, *praying* for me. I didn't consider the girls who look at me as a role model. Suddenly, I feel compelled to explain myself. I pick up the phone in the motel room and am momentarily astonished to find that it actually works. I dial the radio station's 1-888 number and listen to the phone ring and ring.

Just as I'm about to give up, there's a click and I hear the deejay's deep voice.

"Magic 101, thanks for calling," he says. "Do you have a comment about Star Beck?"

"Uh, yes," I say hesitantly.

"Okay," he says. "I'm going to need you to turn down your radio in the background so we don't get feedback on the air. What's your name, caller?"

"Amanda," I say. It feels weird to say it. I reach over and turn the radio off. "I'm calling from St. Petersburg."

"Okay, hang out for a second," the deejay says. There's a pause and then his voice drops an octave. "Hello, and welcome back to Magic 101. We're talking this morning about superstar Star Beck. Is she in rehab? Or is this just one more high-profile celebrity publicity stunt? I have Amanda from St. Pete on the line. Amanda, go ahead."

I try to put on a Southern accent. I don't quite sound as much like Maple as I hoped, though, as I begin talking. "I don't think she's in rehab."

"Then why no public appearance to deny it?" the deejay asks.

"Maybe she has a good reason," I say defensively.

"Like what?" he prompts.

"I don't know," I say, still drawling pathetically. "Like maybe she's just getting really tired of her life, you know? Maybe she feels like she never has a chance to just be herself. Maybe she feels like every single move she makes is controlled and everything she says is scripted. Maybe she just wants to be out of the spotlight for a little while."

The deejay laughs, startling me.

"Yeah, like any of us wouldn't trade places with her in a heartbeat," he says. "C'mon, Amanda. Why would she want to walk away from the lap of luxury? She probably has dozens of little minions running around to wait on her every desire."

I feel a surge of annoyance. "No, she doesn't," I snap.

The deejay sounds amused. "Whoa, Amanda, sounds like you're taking this a little personally here. I guess you're a big fan. But be logical. She's been pampered her whole life. What does she have to escape from?"

"Maybe she feels like her whole life has been a lie," I say.

"Interesting theory," the deejay says, and I know he doesn't mean that at all. "All right, thanks for calling—"

"I bet she feels really bad about the example she's setting for her young fans," I interrupt. "She would probably feel really bad if she knew everyone thought she was in rehab for alcoholism. She's probably really concerned that so many people are worrying about her."

"Amanda, you sound like a nice girl," the deejay says finally with an edge of impatience in his voice. "But you're being awfully naïve. Star Beck has probably never worried about another human being in her life."

★

Chapter 9

I take a quick shower, although the water temperature doesn't go any higher than frigid. I still feel a bit gross as I wrap myself in a tattered towel, but at least I manage to shake the angry feelings I had after the radio call-in.

I put on jeans, a faded Rolling Stones T-shirt and my flip-flops, dab on some concealer to cover the pimple that seems to have materialized on my chin overnight and follow up with some mascara and a swipe of lipstick. Then I slip my glasses on and comb my damp hair back into the Dodgers cap.

It takes a moment for my eyes to adjust to the daylight after I step outside, but when they do, the first thing I notice is the sign in the window of the restaurant next door: BREAKFAST SERVED. I take a deep breath, and an enticingly sweet mixture of bacon, eggs, pancakes and frying grease wafts into my nose. I close the motel room door behind me and cross the parking lot to the restaurant.

Seems like as good a place as any to start my life as a normal Florida girl, right?

The building is painted in faded red, white and green stripes, and a matching canopy hangs over the front entrance. A big signs outside says D'ANGELO'S RISTORANTE in big cursive letters. The parking lot is nearly empty, and as I step through the glass front door, I hear a little chime announcing my arrival.

"Sit anywhere you like!" says the woman who pokes her dark-haired head out from the kitchen just long enough to take a quick look at me. "I'll be with you in a sec!" she adds as her head disappears again.

I look around the restaurant and realize that I'm practically the only person here. The only other customer is a dark-haired guy in a booth against the wall. He's bent over what appears to be a textbook, and I can only see the top of his head as he studies it. There's a steaming mug of coffee beside him.

My heart's pounding. This is it. I'm finally entering my first day in my new home in my new world. I can't screw it up. But what if someone recognizes me? What if I act jittery, like at Mel's Diner? I close my eyes for a moment.

"Be calm," I murmur, realizing that closing my eyes in the entryway to a restaurant probably already qualifies as acting weird. Okay then. I open my eyes and square my shoulders. *Just be normal. No one's looking for you. Everyone thinks you're in rehab in New York.*

I take a deep breath and head toward the back of the restaurant. As I pass the occupied booth, the guy glances up and smiles briefly at me. Right away, I realize he's about my age—maybe a year or two older. He has wire-rimmed glasses, darkly tanned skin, a strong jawline and, when he smiles, straight, white teeth and dimples.

He's cute.

Very cute.

I smile back without thinking, flashing him the big grin I reserve for charming TV hosts during interviews. It works every time, and I fully expect the guy to blush or fumble the pen in his hand or stutter something embarrassing.

But instead, as I glide gracefully past him like the good

little pop star I am, all he does is go back to reading his textbook. He doesn't even give me a second glance as I sit down two booths away. I frown.

What was *that*?

I've never experienced a complete *non*reaction from a guy.

Is this what life as a noncelebrity is like?

Wow.

I mean, it's great that he doesn't recognize me. But what's with him not even *noticing* me? And why is it bothering me so much?

"Good morning," says a voice above me. The dark-haired woman who poked her head out of the kitchen a moment ago is now standing beside my booth, peering down at me. I wonder how long she's been standing there, watching me watch the back of the dark-haired guy's unresponsive head.

"Uh, good morning," I stammer, trying to sound casual.

"Here's a menu," she says, handing me a small laminated book. "Breakfast is on the first page. I'll be back in a moment." She turns and starts to walk away. "You need coffee? Orange juice?"

"Yes," I say. "Um, both please."

"Coming right up," she says cheerfully over her shoulder as she makes her way toward the kitchen. As I begin reading the menu, I notice the dark-haired guy glance quickly over his shoulder at me and then back at his textbook. My heart leaps for a second and then sinks again as I realize his gaze didn't linger on me for more than an instant.

I know I should feel relieved. But instead, I just feel uneasy.

"Know what you want?" the waitress asks without looking at me as she reappears with a silver carafe and pours coffee into a white mug with a blue rim.

I glance down and quickly settle on the bacon, eggs and hash browns combo.

"White toast or wheat?" she asks, jotting down my order.

"Wheat," I say, thinking of my dietician, Jacques. Then I shake my head. Jacques isn't here, is he? "White," I correct myself. "With extra butter."

The waitress stops on the way back to the kitchen at the cute guy's table. She says something to him, and I can see him nod. He laughs as she walks away.

A moment later, I watch as he closes his book, slides out of the booth and stretches. He's taller than I expected—maybe six foot two, which would make him several inches taller than me—and his shoulders are broad. He looks strong. He's dressed in a gray T-shirt, jeans and flip-flops, and I'm just in the middle of thinking what a nice body he has when he turns around. I blush involuntarily and try my best charming smile again.

He looks at me in apparent confusion for a moment and

shoots me a brief, polite (but depressingly unflirtatious) smile. Then he picks up his book and walks out the front door.

For the first time in my life, I've utterly failed to interest a guy.

Well. This is new. Most of me is bummed. But in a way, surprisingly, it actually feels a little good.

After scarfing down my big breakfast, I'm in my ridiculously pink Beetle heading nervously south, toward where my father's store is (according to the old Yellow Pages in my motel room) without a real plan. I'm confused about the fact that my smile has apparently stopped working, and I don't want to spend a second longer in my dingy motel room than I have to. I have to admit to myself that I'm not 100 percent thrilled with the way my first brushes with normalcy are turning out, but I don't want to think I've made a mistake by coming here. It can't be a mistake.

Normal is good, I keep telling myself.

I'm fully aware that I may be delusional.

I drive downtown, heading for 528 Twelfth Avenue South, my heart pounding as I follow a map I bought at a gas station. Mecham's Music. I could try my dad's house first, but I figure that during the day, he'll be at his store, right? As I turn onto Twelfth Street in the downtown area, I begin to scan both sides of the street.

Then I see it. A big sign with an electric guitar and the words MECHAM'S MUSIC: FOR ALL YOUR MUSIC NEEDS soars above the street on the right, atop a large white building set in front of a strip mall.

I'm frozen. This is it. Despite the number of times I've imagined this moment in the past few days—and, honestly, in the last thirteen years—there's something about really, truly being here that makes me feel almost like I want to throw up. But it's not like the occasional pre-concert jitters. Those I can usually shake by reminding myself it's just one night. This time, if I'm not perfect, I could lose my dad forever.

I don't even have a plan.

I take a deep breath and turn right into the parking lot. At this very moment, my father could be just yards away.

I'm in love the second I step inside. Every surface seems to be covered with some sort of instrument. In a room off to the right, there are dozens of electric guitars lined up neatly on stands, and behind them sit a row of equally gleaming acoustic guitars.

Beyond the guitars is a room full of drum-related gear. Off to the left is an area full of pianos and keyboards, and just behind that, there's an organ and two harps. There's a small wind instrument room, and there's another room filled with trumpets, trombones, tubas and sousaphones.

I stop in the sheet music section and pick up the first book I see. It's a piano book that includes the Beatles' greatest hits, and as I absently flip through "Hey Jude" and "Come Together" and "Drive My Car," my eyes dart around the store. I feel certain I'll recognize my father the instant I see him.

"Can I help you?" says a male voice behind me, startling me. I whirl around.

A pimply-faced guy (not that I should talk, now that I'm sporting two enormous zits myself) in a white collared shirt and a nametag that says ZACH looks expectantly at me.

"Er, no, I'm fine," I say.

"Are you sure?" Zach asks eagerly. "Because I'm very familiar with our entire sheet music selection. I'm a musician myself."

I stare at him for a moment, willing him to go away. When he doesn't, I sigh. "Really, I'm fine."

"Are you sure?" he persists.

"Is the owner of the store in?" I ask. Zach pales a bit.

"No," he says quickly. He holds up his hands defensively, palms facing me. "But please don't report me. I'm just trying to help you. Honest."

"I'm not going to report you," I say. "I just wanted to, um, ask him something."

I suspect I don't sound very convincing, but Zach no longer appears to be looking at me with any suspicion.

"Well, Mr. Mecham isn't in today," Zach says. My heart swells at the mention of my dad's name. "But I'm sure that anything he can answer, I can answer for you too," he adds proudly.

Not quite, I feel like saying. *I doubt you can answer whether my father still loves me. I doubt you can answer why he let my mom take me away. I doubt you can answer whether or not I can come live with him for a while or whether we can be a family again.* But instead, I settle for making a random music request.

"Okay. Do you have any sheet music for . . . ," I pause and wonder if it'll be too obvious if I say my own name. Ah, what the heck. Zach obviously doesn't recognize me anyhow. ". . . for Star Beck?" I conclude.

Zach's face brightens, and he looks thrilled to have been asked something he can answer.

"Yep!" He beams. "We've gotten a ton of requests for her stuff lately." He lowers his voice and leans forward, like he's about to tell me a secret. "Do you really think she's in rehab?"

"No, I don't think so," I say as casually as possible.

"Yeah, it's probably just a publicity stunt. Celebrities can never get enough attention."

"Um . . . right," I agree.

"Anyhow," Zach continues, "Mr. Mecham always keeps a good amount of her sheet music in stock."

My heart skips a bit at this. "Why?" I ask tentatively. Zach looks at me like I've sprouted a third eyeball. *Because he loves her*, I imagine Zach saying.

"Duh," he says instead. "Because she's so popular?"

"Oh," I say dumbly. "Right. Of course." *Don't be stupid*, I chide myself as Zach leads me to the pop music section. *It's not like your dad goes around announcing who his long-lost daughter is. That would be weird.*

As we round the row of pop music scores, Zach gestures to a bin of sheet music labeled STAR BECK in big, bold letters. I gulp back a lump in my throat and squeak out a thank-you to Zach who finally, thankfully, gets the hint and walks away.

I turn to face the stack of Star Beck music, *my* music, which makes me feel better than anything else since I ran away. It means my dad has never stopped thinking about me.

"I totally love her, don't you?" The voice snaps me out of my daze. I turn my head to stare at the girl next to me, who looks like she's about twelve. Her hair is up in twin French braids, and she's in a maroon plaid skirt and a white oxford shirt with the name ST. RAPHAEL'S embroidered over the right breast pocket.

"What?" I ask in confusion, not even sure that she's talking to me.

"Star Beck," she says excitedly, gesturing to the sheet music I'm holding dreamily in my hands. "I totally love her. Don't you?"

"I used to," I finally say, looking back and forth from the girl's excited face to the Star Beck songbook she's clutching. On the book's cover, there's a photo of a prerunaway me, and I can't take my eyes off it. My long red curls are blowing behind me in the breeze and I'm gazing off into the distance like I'm looking at something. I'm wearing a flowing white dress that's *almost* see-through—just enough to be suggestive without being revealing. I look content. But I remember that day. And I *wasn't* content. I had just had a fight with Mom about going out that night.

Sarah Swidler, one of my costars on *Secrets of My Teenage Life*, was in town with her boyfriend, and she had wanted me to join them for dinner after the shoot. *No*, Mom said. *You have to practice. You have dance lessons tonight.* I got angry and insisted that I knew my routine. *Can't I take just one* evening *off?* I pleaded. Mom shook her head and looked disappointed in me. *Honestly, Star, I would think you'd* want *to work hard,* she said critically. I remember feeling stung. How could she accuse me of not working hard? Working hard was all I did.

"I hope she's okay," says the pigtailed girl, breaking into my thoughts. "My mom said she's in some alcohol program or something because she drinks too much."

I follow her gaze back to my photo. I look back at the girl, whose eyes are wide and round and concerned.

"I'm sure she's fine," I say, perhaps too confidently. "And I'm sure she doesn't drink." The girl looks at me a bit skeptically.

"How do *you* know?" she asks. I shrug.

"I don't, really," I say. "But I bet she's happier than she was before."

The girl looks at me like I'm crazy.

"If she's rich and famous, why would she need to be happier?" she asks. "Her life must be *perfect.*"

"You'd be surprised." I slowly make my way out of the store, running my hand along the tops of pianos and the necks of guitars as I go, imagining that my father has touched these very instruments. I'm disappointed that he isn't here, but I feel weirdly closer to him than I have in thirteen years.

Okay, so being in my dad's store made me feel all sorts of things—sad, lonely, confused . . . and more than a little desperate. As I walk out to the parking lot, I know I can't wait. I just can't. I wanted to meet him at his store because it seemed more casual, more normal that way. But Zach said he wouldn't be in today. I've waited thirteen years. Suddenly, I don't feel like I can wait another second.

I climb into my car and pull the letter from my father out of my purse. I run my hand lightly over the front. I can almost imagine my father writing it, touching his pen to the envelope, wondering if he'll ever see me again.

"Yes," I say out loud, hoping that somewhere out there, he knows I'm looking for him. "Yes, I'm going to find you."

As I blink back the unexpected tears threatening at the corners of my eyes, I look up and notice two teenage guys hanging out outside the building, looking at me funny. For a moment, I have this sick feeling in the pit of my stomach that they've recognized me. Then I realize they're snickering—probably because I'm a weird girl sitting in a crazy pink car, talking to herself and crying.

"Stop being crazy," I tell myself firmly. I take a deep breath and start the Beetle.

I don't have a plan, exactly. I just know I can't wait any longer.

Fifteen minutes later, I pull up outside my dad's house. It's a little white-trimmed blue cottage, right across from a park with a playground. My heart does a funny flip-flop as I think of what my life would have been like if I had grown up here. Would my father have pushed me on the swings? Would he have played with me?

I get out of the car, noticing the marigolds lining the walkway, the way the grass is a little overgrown but still bright green. The shades of the house are drawn, but as I walk slowly toward the pale blue front door, I imagine what's behind them. Does my dad live here alone? Or did he remarry after my mom? Is there a room for me, just in case I come home one day?

No, I tell myself quickly. *That's stupid. He doesn't know you anymore.*

And he thinks you don't care because you've never written back.

The thought makes me sad.

I stare at the door for a moment before doing anything. Then I steel myself and push the doorbell. I listen carefully for footsteps—my dad's footsteps—but I don't hear any. After a moment, I try again. The bell echoes inside. But after that, there's only silence. I knock a few times. Still nothing.

"They're away, dear!"

A grandmotherly woman is standing out on the lawn next door. She's wearing a robe and has curlers in her hair, and she's watering her roses with a long green hose.

"They won't be back for another two days!" the woman adds pleasantly.

"They?" I ask tentatively. She blinks and takes a step closer to me, still aiming the hose at a row of rosebushes with big red blooms.

"Yes, the Mechams," she says. "Pete, Lynda and their little daughter, Alison."

★

Chapter 10

"**D**aughter?" I repeat. The woman shuts off her hose.

"You *are* looking for the Mechams, right?" she asks.

"Yes," I say after a moment. I'm trying to keep the wobble out of my voice. "Did you say they have a daughter?"

The woman nods. "Alison. She just started kindergarten.

They're just away for the weekend; they'll be back day after tomorrow. Who did you say you were?"

"I'm . . . a family friend," I say. The woman peers at me closely, squinting her eyes.

"You look so much like little Alison," she says, squinting at me. My heart lurches. "I thought you might be a relative," she says.

For a moment, I can't speak.

"I kind of am," I say finally. Then, because I'm afraid of what I might say if I stick around any longer, I thank the woman and hurry back to my car. She watches me until I've rounded the corner out of the neighborhood.

I think I might be sick. I mean, really, truly, I might just throw up in the passenger seat of this old Beetle. I'm shaking as I drive, taking deep breaths, drinking in the air in hungry gulps. I can't seem to get ahold of myself.

Daughter?

He has a daughter?

I have a sister?

I just want you to know that I've never forgotten about you, my dad said in the letter. The words keep playing and replaying in my head. *You are—and always will be—my little girl.*

But am I? He never had the chance to know me. And now he has another little girl, a *real* little girl, who he has probably seen every day of her life.

It occurs to me for the first time, as I drive, that, like Ben said, he might not be what I expect. The thought startles me. The whole daughter thing has totally thrown me for a loop. What if he's *not* happy to see me? What if this Alison has all but replaced me? What if his letters to me were out of habit or guilt or something, not out of loving and missing me?

I feel suddenly frantic, shaken, confused.

What do I do if he doesn't want me after all? What happens to me then? The thought of going back to my mom as a failure makes my stomach twist in knots. But it's not like I can stay in the crappy Star Light Motel much longer. I'm running out of money.

I realize I need a backup plan. I need to learn to be normal on my own, without my dad. Maybe he doesn't want me after all. Somehow, since getting the letter, the thought hasn't occurred to me. But now it feels very real. Scary real.

I realize I need to stand on my own two feet for the first time in my life. I'm just not entirely sure I know how.

I don't need no high heels;
I don't need no
Little black dress.
I travel light on my own time;
I make no excuses
And create my own mess.

—"MY OWN MESS," STAR BECK
ALBUM: *SIMPLY STAR*

★
Chapter 11

The next morning, I wake up with a stomachache, but I'm not sure whether it's from eating an entire Domino's pizza last night or from the fact that my bed is about as comfortable as a sheet of metal. I slowly uncurl my body from the fetal position and pry the Raid canister loose from my right hand. I fell asleep last night clutching it, just in case, since I could have sworn I heard the pitter-patter of little bug feet as I lay in bed.

My feet land on the grimy carpet, and I shudder. I have to get out of this hotel room. Since my father won't be back until tomorrow, I have a whole day to myself. What would a normal person do on a normal day? I rack my brain.

Shopping!

That's it! I'll go to the mall. I'll buy a newspaper to see if there's anything else about me and my supposed stint in rehab in there. I'll get a cup of coffee at Starbucks. I'll look at accessories in real-people stores and shop at Forever 21 instead of Prada. I'll look at shoes at Macy's instead of at Manolo Blahnik.

Sounds like the perfect day. The perfect *normal* day. I hum to myself as I get dressed, trying not to think about my dad and instead thinking about how very *normal* I can be. I take a deep breath.

"I'm ready," I say to no one, "to start my brand-new life."

Except I never make it.

I get directions from the sleepy-looking front-desk guy at the motel, who tells me the closest mall is WestShore Plaza, right across the bridge in Tampa. So I start driving north on Fourth Street. I'm actually in a really good mood.

Until I start to realize that something feels funny about my car. It seems I'm feeling every bump, every crack in the pavement. I don't remember it being this sensitive to the bumps in the road before. I tell myself it's probably nothing and keep driving.

But I've gone less than a half mile more when I begin to see smoke rising from the front right side of the car.

Oh my God! I think. *The engine's on fire! My car's about to explode. They'll find me splattered on the pavement on Fourth Street. They won't recognize me without the red hair, but DNA tests will confirm that it is indeed Star Beck who has met her bitter and tragic end thanks to an exploded car engine in St. Petersburg.*

I'm snapped out of my self-pity by a pickup truck that has pulled up alongside me and has matched my speed. The guy in the passenger seat is gesturing wildly at me. It takes me a moment to realize he's trying to get me to roll down my window.

"You have a flat tire!" he shouts once I finally oblige and put the driver's-side window down. "Pull over!"

Oh. Of course. I knew that.

I slowly brake and steer my car onto the shoulder of the road. I expect the pickup driver to pull in behind me to help, but he just gives me a wave, accelerates and zooms on by!

Great. At least my engine isn't about to explode. I guess I should be thankful for that. There will be no pop star splatterings on Fourth Street today.

I sit there for a moment wondering what to do. I realize I have absolutely no idea. I know it makes me sound really dumb, but honestly, I've never had a car before. Everything's always been taken care of for me. Who are you supposed to call when your car breaks down?

Obviously I need to get help, but where? Maybe someone in the supermarket across the street will know. But getting there turns out to be easier said than done. First, I have to dart across three lanes of fast-moving northbound traffic to get to the median. Then I have to defy death again as I dart across the southbound lanes. I narrowly escape being splattered for the second time today. I'm breathing hard by the time I walk into the Winn-Dixie.

"Hi," I say stupidly as I walk up to the customer service desk. "My car broke down. I mean, my tire. It's flat. Across the street."

The assistant manager behind the desk, who can't be more than a few years older than me, stares at me and shrugs.

"I'll call a tow truck for you," he says. "You got AAA?"

"Why does everyone think I'm in rehab?" I exclaim, frustrated.

He stares at me. "No, not AA." He rolls his eyes. "Triple A. The auto club."

I blush. "Oh. Uh, in that case, no. I don't have AAA."

I actually don't even know what AAA is.

He makes a call, then tells me a tow truck will be there in fifteen minutes. "It'll be expensive, though," he warns.

I feel a knot form in the pit of my stomach. I only have a little over four hundred dollars left.

Twenty-five minutes later, I'm back in the car when a tow truck pulls up behind me. The driver, a middle-aged guy with a big bald spot and low-slung pants under a big belly, hops out, scratching his head, and instead of approaching me in the driver's seat, he goes directly to my flat front tire.

"What'd you do?" he asks gruffly as I step out of the car.

"Uh . . . ," I begin, not knowing what to say. He's already bending down to examine my tire, so I join him. It's now basically just a flat strip of rubber that smells like it's burning.

"You are damned lucky you didn't destroy your rim," he says after a moment of examining the remains of the tire. "You coulda been killed. You shoulda pulled over sooner," he adds. "You got a spare?"

I tell him I'm not sure and he looks at me like I'm crazy.

"How do you own a car and not know if you've got a spare?" he barks. I shrug, embarrassed.

"I just bought the car a few days ago," I explain sheepishly.

Grumbling under his breath, the driver asks for my key and goes to the *front* of my car.

"I thought you said you just needed the tire," I say, wondering why he's about to lift the hood.

He stares at me like I'm crazy. "In old Beetles, the *trunk* is in the front of the car," he said slowly. "The *engine*'s in the back."

"Oh" is all I say.

He rolls his eyes and opens my trunk (which *is* in the front, as it turns out), where, thankfully, he does find a spare and a jack. I watch in astonishment as he quickly raises the car with the jack, loosens the wasted tire, removes it and puts the narrow spare on. Then he stands up and dusts his hands off against his jeans.

"You're good to go," he says. "That'll be a hundred seventy-five dollars for the service call. You should have AAA. Would have saved you some serious cash."

"I've heard," I grumble. I hand over the money, in cash, and feel very uneasy as I realize this leaves me with only about $225. He hands me the keys to my car. "But you can't go more than a few miles on this. Are you headed far?"

I sigh. Obviously I'll have to kiss the mall trip goodbye. No money for Forever 21 now. Darn it.

"No." I shake my head and point down the street, back in the direction of the horrid motel. "Just another mile or two back down Fourth Street."

"You should be able to make it, then, if you drive slow," the driver says. "But you need to get yourself to a tire dealership. You got to get a real tire on that wheel. You can't drive far on a spare. They're not built for mileage."

"Oh," I say, my heart sinking.

The driver jots something down on a piece of paper, which he hands to me.

"Here's directions to a tire dealership we do a lot of business with on Fourth," he says. "A new tire there should run you about a hundred and fifty bucks, including the labor, if you get a decent one."

"Thanks," I say, already doing the mental math and starting to feel totally hopeless.

"Drive safe now," the driver adds over his shoulder as he turns to walk back toward his truck. He pulls away with a screech of rubber against pavement.

I'm completely out of my element the moment I pull into the tire dealership. I have no idea what to do. "Hello," I say as I approach the counter. "My tire is broken."

The man behind the counter arches an eyebrow at me. He's tall with sandy hair and a thick beard that reminds me of Wolverine from the X-Men.

"Your tire is *broken*?" he repeats dubiously, looking me up and down.

"Yes," I say, feigning confidence. "I mean, I was driving today, and it broke."

"It's flat, you mean," Wolverine says, looking amused.

"Yes, flat," I confirm, wondering why I seem to be amusing him. "Anyhow, so I need a new tire, I guess."

"It's pretty standard to buy tires in pairs so that both tires on an axle match," he says. I feel myself pale.

"Two tires?" I ask. "How much?"

"Depends on the type you need. What kind of car do you have?"

I tell him, and he walks outside, where he bends down and looks at the tires on my car. He comes back in and jots a few things down; then he enters some information into his computer.

"One tire, with labor, taxes and service, comes to $179.56."

I stare at the figure, take a deep breath and sign in the blank he indicates.

One hundred eighty bucks—great.

He tells me it will take about an hour. As I walk slowly to the waiting area and sit down in front of the fuzzy TV, which is turned to *The Jerry Springer Show*, I feel a slight sense of panic set in.

The tire purchase will wipe out most of my cash. I'll have less than fifty dollars left.

Who would have thought that a multimillionaire would be worrying about how to scrape by from one day to the next? I'm so lost in thought that I don't even notice someone sit down across from me until he speaks.

"Hey, you're the girl from the restaurant, aren't you?"

I look up and see, to my astonishment, that Cute Textbook Boy is sitting across the waiting area from me. He's wearing a gray T-shirt and dark jeans, and his hair is sort of messed up, but in a way that makes him look even hotter than he did at the restaurant. I gape at him. Actually, I almost fall off my chair. I think I gurgle some kind of response that doesn't consist of actual words.

"You okay?" he asks after a moment.

"Um, yeah," I say, collecting myself. I straighten up in my chair, push my glasses up and pull my cap down. I blink at him a few times. I can't believe he's here. Or that he recognized me. Well, not *me*, exactly. But the Amanda version of me. The new me.

He leans forward and smiles. Sheesh, those dimples. Those perfect teeth. That olive skin. I can't deal.

"I recognized your Dodgers hat," he says. "Not many Dodgers fans around here."

I can't get my tongue to cooperate and say anything.

"I'm sorry. I didn't mean to bother you. I just got here to pick my truck up, and they told me five more minutes. I can go wait over there if you want," Cute Textbook Boy says after a minute, looking at me uncertainly.

"No," I say quickly. "I mean, that's fine. Stay here. I was just, um, thinking."

"About what?" Cute Textbook Boy asks. He studies my face, and I fight the urge to gaze dreamily back into his eyes. I look quickly away. After all, I can't have people looking too closely at me, right? Especially when their looking at me makes my heart race.

"Just money," I blurt out. "I mean, after I pay for this tire, I have, like, no money left."

I feel like crying. And I realize I probably sound like a total idiot, blurting out personal information like that. Something is happening to my brain.

"Do you have a job?" he asks. "To earn money for the tire, I mean?"

"No."

He looks like he's about to say something, but just then, the mechanic behind the desk barks out, "Green Jeep Cherokee?" and looks in our direction. Cute Textbook Boy stands up.

"That's me." He shrugs. "Look, you should apply at D'Angelo's," he says. "They're hiring."

"The restaurant?" I ask stupidly, my mind spinning. Me? Work at a restaurant? I can't even imagine. But it would be a job. And maybe I'd get to see Cute Textbook Boy more often. Now, *that* would be worth thinking about.

"Yeah," he says. "You know, menus, pasta, customers . . ."

"Got it," I say, laughing. "Thanks."

"Sure," he says. He looks at me for another moment. "Anyhow, um, see you around."

He's gone before I realize that I didn't even get his name.

By the time my car's done an hour later, I've thought it through. I don't have a choice. My money will run out soon, which means just one thing.

Cute Textbook Boy is right. I have to get a job.

Twenty minutes later, I'm scarfing down a pepperoni calzone, feeling illogically disappointed that Cute Textbook Boy isn't here, when the dark-haired waitress arrives at my table to see if I'd like a refill on my drink.

"Yes," I say, "but I also have a question."

"Yes?" she asks as she pours me more Coke from the pitcher in her hand. I take a breath.

"I heard you're hiring," I begin. I draw a deep breath and add, "I'd like to apply."

She raises an eyebrow at me.

"To be a waitress here?" she asks dubiously.

"Yes," I say with as much confidence as I can muster, which actually isn't much at all. She looks at me for a second.

"Do you have waitressing experience?" she asks.

"Yes," I say firmly, although it's a complete lie. Well, not completely. I have lots of experience being waited *on*. How hard can it be?

She regards me critically for a moment.

"How old are you?" she asks.

"Eighteen," I say instantly. I have no idea how it works to get a job when you're underage, but I don't want to find out the hard way, thank you very much. I draw myself up a little straighter in the booth, trying to look as adult as possible.

"Well, I'm pretty desperate for the help," she says. She sets the Coke pitcher down. "See, my cousin Mario, who was one of the waiters and an assistant manager, eloped yesterday with Jenny, one of my most reliable waitresses. They both just up and quit!" She throws her hands in the air to punctuate her statement.

"That's too bad," I say. The woman shakes her head.

"I'm Bev D'Angelo," she says, extending her hand. "My husband Louie and I own this place."

"Oh, I didn't realize you were the owner," I say, shaking her hand.

She nods. "So you say you have experience?"

"Yes. And I'm easy to train," I add. After all, I don't want her having any reason to not hire me.

She smiles at me. "Can you start this afternoon?"

I gulp. "Okay." I hadn't *exactly* expected to start my new career so soon.

"Great!" she says. "I'll put you on the books, and we'll take care of the tax stuff later. Besides, most of your income will come from tips anyhow. There is one thing I need to know now, though."

I blink.

"Your name?" she says with a laugh.

"Oh! It's . . . Amanda," I tell her.

"Amanda what?" she asks. I can't say Beckendale. Not when all you have to do is Google *Amanda Beckendale* and a thousand entries for *the real name of Star Beck* pop up. My eyes rove around the table.

"Pepper!" I say.

"Amanda Pepper?" she repeats. Okay, it sounds a bit weird. But Pepper could be a last name. Right?

"Okay then," Bev says, wiping her hands on her apron. She checks her watch, then picks up the pitcher of Coke she set on the corner of my table. "Pleased to meet you, Amanda Pepper. Can you be back here in two hours? That'll give me an hour to train you on our system here before we open for dinner at four. Does that work for you?"

127

"Sure. And thanks," I say as she smiles and walks back to the kitchen. "You just got your first real job," I say to myself in awe.

★

Waiting tables isn't as easy as it looks. Actually, it's next to impossible. I've never felt so stupid in my entire life.

Who knew that living a pampered pop-star life would leave me so completely unprepared for reality?

"We want two glasses of water and a bottle of Chianti," says the large, pockmarked, artificially redheaded woman seated in my first booth. Her voice is nasal and she's with a rail-thin, hollow-eyed man who doesn't make a peep. I nod and write it down on my pad, then I look back at her, wondering if she wants to order an appetizer or anything. She stares at me.

"What are you waiting for?" she demands after a moment. "We're thirsty!"

I feel silly and quickly apologize. I'm back in the kitchen before I realize that I have no idea what Chianti is. I grab a menu and flip it open. I scan the beverages and realize it's a red wine. Okay, red wine. No problem. I scan the bottles on the shelf in the back until I see one that says *Chianti*. See, this is easy.

I bring out the glasses of water first; then I return with two wineglasses; then I finally come back with the bottle of wine. Bev stops me on the way and whispers, "You can use a tray, you know. It will hurry things along."

Right. A tray. I set the wine bottle on the table, smile and say, "Here you go. I hope you like it. I'll be back in a moment to take your order."

I've just started to walk away, feeling impressed with myself for completing this first task so successfully, when I hear the woman's nasal voice calling out behind me.

"Waitress!" she squawks. "Where are you going? Aren't you going to open the wine?"

I have to open it? I paste a pleasant smile on my face and return to the table.

"Of course," I say brightly. I pick up the bottle and look at it, then peel off the paper that's around the cap. Except, there's no screw cap. The neck of the bottle is stuffed with a cork.

"It's a cork," I say dumbly, looking at the bottle in confusion. The woman just stares at me.

I have no idea how to open a bottle of wine. Luckily, Bev does.

"Sorry, Amanda." Bev comes over with a small metal gadget. "I must have forgotten to give you a corkscrew." She deftly inserts the gadget into the cork, twists a few times and pulls. The bottle pops open, and she pours two glasses. The woman grumbles something under her breath and takes a big sip of the wine. Bev puts a hand on my shoulder and leads me away. "Some of our customers can be a little grumpy," she says. "You'll get used to it. Just don't let them get to you."

Two hours later, they've gotten to me. We're in the middle of the dinner rush, and my night is only getting worse. I'm so embarrassed and flustered that I can barely function anymore.

I screwed up the order of the Fat Lady–Quiet Man couple and brought them two spaghetti and meatballs when they had actually asked for one spaghetti and meatballs and one lasagna (or so the woman claimed). With my next table, I mixed up the Coke and Diet Coke in my hands and wound up giving the man the diet and the woman the regular, which of course they complained about. Oops. Moments later, I brought two teenagers a delicious-looking green pepper and mushroom pizza when they had actually asked for jalapeño peppers and olives.

Bev is still pleasant, but I also don't think it's my imagination that she's looking at me a bit skeptically now too. I'm sure she's starting to wonder exactly what kind of waitressing experience I've actually had, since I can't seem to get even simple things right. She's probably preparing to fire me any moment now.

That's why I'm relieved—for a split second, at least— when I return to the kitchen a few minutes after the botched pizza delivery and she asks me to deliver some drinks to one of Amber's tables, since Amber is busy trying to ring someone's order up right now. I cheerfully agree and ask what drinks they need.

"They're already poured," Bev says, barely paying attention to me. She's typing something into a calculator and looks lost in thought. "They're over there. I already loaded them onto a tray for you. They go to table thirty-four, the big table in back. There's a party of ten there. You can't miss 'em."

My heart sinks as I look at the tray, loaded with ten glasses that are full to the rims with ice and soda.

"Sure," I say weakly. This will take a while. I grab two of the drinks and start to head out of the kitchen.

"Hold on!" Bev calls behind me. "Amanda, just take the tray. You can't serve ten drinks two by two."

"Of course not," I say sheepishly. I backtrack, put the drinks back on the tray, and stare down at it. I can't possibly carry it. Can I?

Okay, deep breaths.

I have great balance, I tell myself. *After all, I'm a great dancer, and my Pilates instructor works with me on my core strength every week.* I know I have poise; the modeling instructor I had as a preteen drilled the whole stand-up-straight-with-your-shoulders-back thing into my head long ago, and I haven't forgotten it. And thanks to my workouts with Gunner, my arms are a lot stronger than they look. Logically, I *should* be able to carry the tray without a problem.

I'm just not so sure that it will actually happen that way.

I take a deep breath, struggle to pick up the tray full of drinks and only slosh them around a little bit. I stand there unsteadily for a moment, nestling the tray against my right shoulder, supporting it with my left hand. Okay, this isn't so bad. I can do this. Hooray, I'm a real waitress!

As I walk slowly into the restaurant, I'm feeling much better. Why did I doubt myself, anyhow? Maybe this whole tray-carrying thing isn't so bad after all. Sure, my arm is starting to ache, and the tray feels a little wobbly, but I only have a few more yards to go before I get there. I'm going to make it. I glance down to make sure that the path ahead of me is clear. And suddenly, I stop in my tracks.

He's here. Cute Textbook Boy is here. Sitting in the same booth as last time.

He's just to my right. I'm practically standing on top of him. I was so focused on waitressing that I almost forgot about him.

He looks more adorable than ever, which of course is

immediately distracting. His dark hair is just a little bit wavy, and it curls gently over his ears. He has one curl that has escaped from the rest and has fallen haphazardly across his forehead. His eyes behind his wire-rimmed glasses are a rich, chocolaty brown. And as he reads his textbook, his forehead is creased just a little, as if he's thinking really hard. I feel a bit weak in the knees. I'm frozen to the spot.

I don't even realize I'm staring until one of the kids from table thirty-four yells, "Are those our drinks?"

I look up, startled, and when I glance back down at Cute Textbook Boy, he's staring right at me. Uh-oh. Busted.

I look at him for a moment, embarrassed. He stares back, and after a second, he grins.

"Hey," he says, dimples appearing at the corners of his mouth.

"Hey," I squeak back. I can't believe he has finally noticed me. My arms feel suddenly weak.

Uh-oh, I think. Then I promptly drop the entire tray of ten icy drinks directly on him.

> You see, my problem is this:
> I'm thinking of you,
> Dreaming of the way you'll kiss
> me.
> I look in your eyes.
> Can't you see I'm looking for a
> sign?
> I don't know how you feel.
> Baby, baby, no, no.
>
> —"HOW YOU FEEL," STAR BECK
> ALBUM: *SECRETS OF A STAR*

★

Chapter 12

"*I* ...am...so...sorry."

Thanks to my complete and utter humiliation, I can barely force the words out of my mouth. I know I've turned as red as the collared shirt I'm wearing as I stand there, open-mouthed, staring at Cute Textbook Boy, who is currently dripping with soda. He has ice in his wavy hair. Even his long eyelashes have droplets of soda hanging from them. The now-empty glasses are rolling around on the table and on the floor. And the whole restaurant is looking. I feel like I could die on the spot.

"Don't worry about it," he says finally, looking back up at me. He's wearing kind of a half grin along with several gallons of soda.

Drip, drip, drip. The liquid drops off him in fat splotches. I'm mortified.

"No, I . . . ," I begin, but I don't know what to say. "I am just so embarrassed. I'm not used to trays and . . ." I clamp my mouth shut after a moment as I realize that I'm babbling and that Cute Textbook Boy probably couldn't care less how familiar I am with trays. He probably just cares that the crazy girl with the weird-colored hair and bad glasses stared at him strangely and then randomly threw a tray of sodas at him.

"Really, it's fine," he says, using his napkin to wipe his face. He shrugs. "I needed a shower anyhow."

That's when I notice that he doesn't look angry. In fact, he's actually *laughing*. And grinning at me with those white teeth and those crazy dimples.

"Seriously, it's no big deal," he says. He slides out of the booth. "Here, let me help you clean up."

"N-n-no," I stutter in surprise. Now he wants to *help* me? "I can do it," I say quickly, bending down to start picking up glasses. "I've already gotten you wet enough."

"I really don't mind," he says, bending down beside me and grabbing a glass.

"I see you've met my son," says a voice above us. We both turn and I slowly look up to see Bev, her hands on her hips as she regards the mess I've made.

"Your son?" I repeat weakly, looking from her to Cute Textbook Boy, who shrugs.

"Actually, Ma, we haven't officially met," he says. He stands, and I slowly straighten up beside him.

Bev sighs. "Amanda, this is Nick. Nick, this is Amanda," she says. "And Nick, it looks to me like Amanda has some cleaning up to do."

Nick shakes my hand in greeting; then I shoot him an embarrassed glance and stand up to look at Bev.

"I am *so* sorry, Bev," I say. I can feel tears prickling the backs of my eyes, and I blink them away. "I don't know what happened. I just . . . I screwed up, and I am so sorry. Can you forgive me?"

"Honey, it's not a matter of forgiving you," Bev says wearily. "I'm just afraid that you're not qualified to do this."

I take a deep breath and start to protest, but Bev puts a finger to her lips.

"Come on," Bev says, putting her arm around my shoulder. She leads me to the kitchen and yells back to ask Lauren and Gillian, two of the other waitresses, to help clean up and get the table of ten some new drinks. Amber shoots me a pitying glance on her way past.

"Honey, have you really waitressed before?" Bev asks once we've arrived back in the kitchen.

I sigh. "No," I admit. I feel terrible.

"Okay," she says, as if she's thinking. "Then maybe this isn't the best situation for you," she says. I can't believe she's not mad. She just seems disappointed.

"But . . . ," I protest, my voice trailing off. But what? I've lied about my lack of experience. I've embarrassed myself—and the restaurant. "But I need the job," I finally mumble. That, at least, is the truth.

Bev sighs and thinks about it for a moment. She pinches the skin above the bridge of her nose with her thumb and forefinger and looks lost in thought.

"I could train her, Ma."

Nick is standing there in the doorway to the kitchen, drying his hair with a dish towel.

"Nicky, I don't know . . . ," Bev says.

"I waited tables in high school." He turns to me. "I don't mind showing you a few things. Including how to balance a tray full of drinks." He grins, and I feel my face heat up again.

"That would be great," I mumble. We both look at Bev. She looks back and forth between us and finally sighs.

"Okay," she agrees. "One more chance, Amanda."

"Thank you," I say. She pats me on the shoulder and gets up to leave the kitchen.

"Amanda?" she says from the doorway. I turn and look at her. "Take the rest of the night off, okay? Maybe Nicky can show you the ropes after the restaurant closes. I'll need you back here at four tomorrow."

"Thank you," I say as she pushes through the swinging doors back to the restaurant.

I turn slowly back to Nick. "Why did you offer to do that?"

"You said you needed the job," he says. "Besides," he adds with a wink, "if I'm going to keep coming here to study, I can't risk being doused by a tray full of drinks again."

I smile at him, and just when I'm thinking we're sharing a moment, he turns away and says, "Meet me back here at eleven tonight and we'll go over some stuff."

Then he disappears back into the restaurant.

I have four hours to kill before I'm due back at D'Angelo's. I'm strangely nervous. I mean, obviously it's not like my after-closing meeting with Nick is a date or anything. But he's gorgeous. He's sweet. And he doesn't seem to hate me, even though I dumped soda all over him. In just a few hours, I'll be alone with him in the restaurant. Is it wrong that that makes my heart beat just a little bit faster? Is it wrong that I can't wipe the smile off my face?

I slowly walk into my motel room, barely glancing at the roach family that scatters as I flip the light on. I grab the can of Raid and absentmindedly spray the chemical killer in their general direction. I'm pretty sure I haven't gotten them, considering that I can still hear them moving around, but for once, I don't care.

"What do I do?" I absently ask the roaches. "Maybe he kind of likes me. I mean, I think I like him. It's just weird. I mean, what am I supposed to talk about with him? It's not like I can tell him who I am. And there's really nothing else interesting about me, is there?"

I miss my old life more than I thought I would. For all the things I hated about it, I never took enough time to look at the things I actually liked. Such as not having to carry trays full of drinks to tables of ten while not knowing how to flirt with cute guys reading textbooks. Sleeping in five-star hotel rooms every night instead of dingy, roach-infested motels. Not having to worry about money—or flat tires or canisters of Raid or how to balance a tray of drinks.

In my old life, guys *wanted* to talk to me. I didn't have to be charming or witty or anything. I just had to *be*, because I was Star Beck. That was enough.

But in this world, the world where I'm suddenly the

klutzy, clueless Amanda Pepper, no one falls in love with me just because I'm standing there.

Suddenly, I'm plain. Boring. Average. And although I know it's what I wanted, I'm not so sure I like it.

I'm back at D'Angelo's at eleven p.m. sharp, feeling strangely more nervous than I do before I go onstage. I go in just before they lock the doors, and I wait for Nick in the entryway, not sure that I'm even allowed back in the kitchen at the moment. I imagine I must not be the most popular person in the restaurant right now, seeing as how I created a scene—as well as a mess that Lauren and Gillian had to clean up.

I admit to spending more time than I should have in front of the mirror before coming here, playing with my hair and using what little makeup I have to make myself look more presentable. Although I'm accustomed to Kim doing my makeup, I managed to do a decent job of figuring out how to partially conceal my zits with foundation and how to layer on the powder and blush appropriately. I used a bit of pale pink lipstick on my eyelids too, and I'm actually pleased with how they shimmer a bit when I blink behind my glasses. With mascara as a finishing touch—and with my messy hair combed back into a cute pony-tail—I actually feel like I look decent. Not Star Beck decent, but average-person decent.

Nick comes out from the back of the restaurant. He has changed shirts and now looks even cuter in a yellow and green USF Bulls tee that has a picture of the university's mascot.

"Is that where you go to school?" I ask, pointing at his shirt.

"Huh?" he asks, then he looks down at his chest. "Oh, yeah," he says when he realizes what I'm pointing at. "The St. Pete campus. I'm a freshman there. Double majoring in economics and Spanish."

"Oh," I say, not knowing where to go from there. I don't know anything about economics. Or Spanish. I suddenly feel really dumb. My singing career seems shallow next to what he's doing. Not that I can tell him about it.

Nick is quiet for a minute and then rakes his hand through his black, wavy hair.

"Where do you go?" he asks. "USF too? Or are you at SPC?"

I have no idea what the letters mean, but either way the answer is no.

"Nowhere right now," I say.

"Are you still in high school?" Nick asks.

"No," I answer honestly, realizing that if I'm claiming to be eighteen, I can't exactly be in the tenth grade. "I've graduated." And I have. If you count my GED.

"Well, are you planning to go to college?" Nick asks, looking a bit concerned. Little does he know I already make more in a month than many people make in a lifetime. I take a deep breath and smile.

"Yes, of course," I say sweetly. It's not a complete lie. I *would* like to take some college classes someday, although I'm not sure that would be possible with my schedule and the fact that everywhere I go as Star Beck, I attract a screaming crowd, which would probably just be annoying to other people on a college campus. "I'm just taking a semester off," I hear myself add. It sounds reasonable, even if it's not entirely true. But I can't have Nick thinking I'm a slacker.

"Okay, Nicky, Dad and I are going to take off," says Bev, startling me as she emerges from the kitchen. "Make sure you lock everything up and turn off the lights before you go to bed."

"Sure, Ma, I know," Nick says, leaning forward to kiss her on the cheek. His father, Louie, an older version of Nick, emerges from the kitchen.

"Good luck," he says as they walk out. With one final wave, Bev locks the door behind them. We're alone in the restaurant.

Nick turns to me, looking almost sheepish.

"Yeah, so, I admit it, I live at my parents' restaurant," he says, as if it's something to be embarrassed about. "Or in the little apartment above it, anyhow. I wanted to live near campus, but we couldn't afford it. Not with the restaurant and all. We're barely breaking even."

I shrug. "I live with my mom too," I say, neglecting to mention that when we're not on the road, she lives at *my* house, not the other way around. "Or I *did*," I amend. "Until very recently."

"Who do you live with now?" he asks curiously.

"By myself," I say. Nick opens his mouth and looks like he's about to ask more, but then he closes it again and nods.

"Right," he says, shaking his head. "Let's get to it, then."

As it turns out, the ability to execute complicated choreographed moves onstage and to contort my body into all sorts of weird positions in the process doesn't directly translate into any sort of grace or poise when carrying a tray full of drinks.

"Amanda, you have to *concentrate*," Nick says patiently after I've dropped yet another tray.

"I'm trying," I say, casting him an apologetic look.

And I *am* trying. Really. And I suspect that eventually, I won't be so bad at this. It's just that there's something about Nick's mere presence that's making me shaky.

But I'm not about to tell him that.

"Okay, let's start smaller," Nick says as we squat on the floor, mopping up the six most recent glasses of water I've dropped. His elbow brushes mine and we lock eyes for a moment. He clears his throat and looks quickly away. "Let's see how you do carrying just two drinks on the tray," he adds.

For the next hour, Nick talks me through balancing the tray properly, keeping my eyes ahead without twisting the tray, keeping my balance with a heavy tray weighing me down and even stacking the tray so that it's less likely to topple over.

"You're doing great," Nick says after I've successfully made three trips across the room with six glasses of water on my tray. I grin at him proudly. This somehow feels better than earning Lance Mojave's approval for my dance steps. "Now let's try eight glasses," Nick says.

"Eight?" I croak.

"Eight," he confirms. "You can do it."

We stand side by side at the counter in the kitchen, our shoulders touching a little. Nick fills two additional glasses with water and leans over to put them on my tray.

Then he helps me hoist the tray up on my shoulder and balance it again. I walk out into the dining room, stroll back and forth twice and then make my way proudly back to the kitchen.

"I did it!" I say.

"Way to go!" exclaims Nick. He claps, like I've just given some kind of great performance. Which I guess I have. I'm still balancing the tray and grinning at him like an idiot when he takes a step closer and touches the small of my back gently. "I'm proud of you, Amanda," he says. But I barely hear him; I can feel the heat from his fingers, and my skin tingles.

Our eyes meet. I don't have much experience with this, but I could swear that I feel a spark between us. There's *something* between us. I know it. All of a sudden, the craziest question pops into my head: *What would it feel like to kiss him?* I can't believe I just thought that. My heart pounds. And suddenly, I forget I'm supposed to be balancing the tray, which is bad news considering that I'm holding eight drinks—and Nick is directly in my line of fire.

For the second time that night, I drop an entire tray full of drinks on him.

After drying off (Nick) and cleaning up (me), Nick proceeds to give me a few quick pointers on restaurant shorthand, such as how to jot down a customer's order without writing the whole thing (*S&MB*, for example, is shorthand for spaghetti and meatballs, and *Ck* is for Coke) and the meanings of certain numbers, such as 86, which means that a restaurant is out of something. As in, "We're eighty-sixed on olives."

While he explains things to me, he asks me questions too. I know I should feel flattered. But instead, I feel nervous, because he's asking things I can't answer without giving too much away.

"So where are you from?" he asks as he jots down several shorthand phrases for common menu items.

"California, near Los Angeles," I say without thinking about it.

"Really?" Nick looks up at me, a surprised expression on his face. "What brought you to Florida, then?"

I think about this for a moment, not sure what to say. Running away? Searching for the long-last parent I haven't seen since I was three? Trying to figure out how to just be normal? No, none of those will *quite* accomplish the whole incognito goal. Instead, I settle for saying, "My father."

"Your father?" Nick asks curiously. "He lives here?"

I nod.

"What does he do?" Nick asks.

"Owns a store," I say simply.

"That's cool," he says, brightening a bit. "Like my parents. So you know what it's like."

"Uh, yeah," I say, neglecting to mention that I actually have no idea what it's like, as I haven't seen my dad in more than a decade.

"Where did you go to high school?" he asks.

"Back in California," I say hurriedly, hating that I have to lie to him. But what am I going to say? *Yeah, I was home-schooled on my tour bus.* I don't think so. "You wouldn't know it."

"Try me," Nick says cheerfully. "I have some friends in L.A."

"Uh," I stall. "Sweet Valley High," I say the first thing that comes to mind and again resist the urge to immediately smack my idiot self in the forehead. Nick looks at me funny.

"Amanda," Nick says slowly. "That's a series of books."

"Which they named after my school," I say quickly, not meeting his eye.

"Listen," Nick says after a minute. Whatever was between us a few minutes ago seems to have disappeared. "We should call it a night. I have class in the morning. And you must be pretty beat."

I yawn. "Yeah," I say, trying not to look as disappointed as I feel. "What I wouldn't give for a deep-tissue massage." Then I clap my hand over my mouth. When I said that, I was thinking of the weekly massages I received when I was on the road. But it couldn't have sounded that way to Nick. He probably thought I was suggesting *he* give me a massage! A deep red flush spreads over my cheeks.

"So do you need a ride home or something?" Nick asks.

I point toward the deserted parking lot. "No, I have a car. An old Beetle."

Nick's eyes twinkle. "So you're the proud owner of those pink wheels." Even though I'm living just next door, I made a point of driving my car to D'Angelo's.

"They were all out of the purple ones," I say. Then it hits me—I'm actually making small talk with a guy. My nerves kick in.

"I should go," I say, shuffling my feet.

Nick takes a few steps closer to me until we're just inches apart. He looks down at me, and my heart beats wildly. He's close enough to touch. Close enough to kiss.

Instead, he holds the door open. "Well, drive safe."

"You too," I say, walking out before it hits me that he's not driving anywhere. "Arghhh!" I say, tapping my head against the steering wheel. I shake off my embarrassment and pull out of the lot.

I have got to put Nick out of my mind. After all, tomorrow is the day my dad should be back. And really, who cares about some random restaurant guy when I'm about to piece back together a whole part of my family that I thought was lost to me forever?

★

Chapter 13

*I*t's ten a.m. on the dot as I get out of my car in the Mecham's Music parking lot. My heart is pounding so hard that I'm worrying again about the possibility of a heart attack. But I can only think about one thing: I'm about to see my dad.

I stride inside, trying to pump myself full of confidence. The first person I see is Zach, the salesguy from the other day, who rolls his eyes at me and says somewhat sourly, "Ah, *you* again. Mr. Mecham's in the guitar room, since you want to see him so much."

Too excited to even thank him, I nod quickly and walk across the store to the guitar room, resisting the urge to run. I recognize the back of my father's head as soon as I round the corner.

His thick brown hair has grayed and thinned over the years, and his once-straight posture is no longer quite as erect, but there's no doubt about it.

It's my dad. My father.

He's dressed in a green shirt and khakis with brown shoes, and his shoulders are just slightly rounded. He's hunched over a guitar and seems deep in thought.

I walk up behind him. "Hi," I say in a voice that doesn't sound like my own.

He turns, our eyes meet, and I suck in an involuntary breath. For a long moment, I'm frozen on the spot, lost in the familiarity of him. His eyes are still the same pale ocean green mine are. He still has the scar I remember over his left eyebrow and the bump on the bridge of his nose. He's gained some weight since I last saw him, and he has crow's-feet and wrinkles he never had before, but seeing him for the first time since I was three instantly takes me back.

"Hi," he says in return, smiling at me. "Can I help you with something?"

There's not a hint of recognition in his eyes, which I suppose shouldn't surprise me, if I'm going to be realistic about things. After all, it *has* been thirteen years.

But now he's looking at me expectantly, probably wondering why I'm standing there gaping at him.

"It's me," I finally squeak out softly.

He squints at me and lights up. "Oh, right!" he says. "You're the one Zach told me about. The one who was asking for me the other day. Is there something I can do to help you?"

This isn't how this moment was supposed to go. I slowly take off my glasses and stare at him, hoping that I'll look more like *me* without them, willing him to look at me and see the little girl he lost years ago.

"Don't you recognize me?" I finally ask in a near whisper. Of course he doesn't. I don't even know why I'm asking.

"Weren't you in here last week, asking about guitars? Sorry I didn't recognize you right away. Welcome back. What can I do for you?"

I stammer out the first question I can think of. "Um, which guitar is better, a Gibson or a Fender?" I blurt out.

"Well, that depends what you're looking for," he says. He walks over to the wall and touches the neck of a Fender. "Now, this one we actually have a sale on right now," he says. He indicates a Gibson. "But this baby is worth every cent too. Do you play?"

"Yes," I answer in a strained whisper. I feel tremendously sad all of a sudden. Seeing him in person like this is driving home the point that I've lost thirteen whole years—almost all my life—with him.

"Great!" he booms, oblivious to the fact that I'm about a second away from bursting into tears. "That's terrific. It's nice to see a gal take up guitar. Now, you know we offer lessons, right?"

"Do you teach them?" I mumble hopefully, thinking I might just sign up if it means nailing down a time and place to see him again. I realize I can't just spring who I am on him. I need more time.

He laughs. "Nah, not me. I'm a piano man myself. My daughter's the guitar player in the family," he says proudly.

I almost throw my arms around him until he adds, "Alison's only six, and she can already play the first few chords of 'Stairway to Heaven.' Can you imagine?"

His new daughter from the life that doesn't include me. It's like I never even existed.

"That's great," I manage to say weakly. My father nods enthusiastically and reaches into his back pocket. He pulls out a flyer, which he hands to me.

"We do a weekly talent show at Muggs, a coffee bar near here. It's an open-mic night kind of thing. It's really worth coming to check out if you're interested in lessons. Maybe you can even play us a little something on guitar. It'll help me to figure out what level you're at. You know any songs?"

"Um, yes," I say, glancing at the flyer. I don't have the heart to tell him that, in fact, I know *hundreds* of songs. And that millions of people in America know my songs too.

"Great!" my father exclaims. "It's settled, then. Come on in. It's tomorrow night. We'll chat there, okay? We'll figure out then what kind of lessons you'll need and we'll get you signed up."

I nod slowly and let him walk me toward the door of the store. I'm in a daze; I feel numb, and as he leads me out, chattering pleasantly, I feel like I've been run over by a semi.

"I didn't catch your name," he says as he opens the door for me.

"Amanda," I say, looking up at him with a glimmer of hope, just in case hearing his daughter's given name rings any bells. But still, nada.

"I'm Pete Mecham," he says pleasantly. He claps me on the back like we're old chums, and I force a smile. "Thanks for coming in, Amanda," he adds, holding the door open for me to walk out.

"Yeah," I say. I wait until I'm back in the car to begin crying.

The tears don't stop for a very long time.

I go through the motions of waiting tables that night. Nick was a good teacher, and I'm vastly improved from last night. Still, I know it's obvious to everyone at the restaurant that something is wrong. Bev pulls me aside twice, and although I reassure her that I'm totally fine, I can see her shooting me furtive glances of concern every time she thinks I'm not looking.

As I hurry back and forth from the kitchen, putting in orders for salads, delivering steaming plates of veal marsala and chicken parmigiana, filling glasses full of ice and soda and clearing dishes away, all I can think about is my father.

For the last thirteen years, my dad's always been there in my head, just beneath the surface. Onstage, when I was younger and got nervous during shows sometimes, I would think about my dad and feel instantly soothed. When I started playing piano, I would think about the days I spent sitting next to him on the piano bench in our old living room, watching him play. My memories of him were all fragments, short movie clips of our time together, but they were always on my mind, replaying in an endless loop.

I could have picked his face out of a crowd of a thousand,

or even a million. I would have known him anywhere. I would have recognized him with glasses or with dyed hair. I would have recognized him if he'd put on a hundred pounds or grown a beard or had a nose job like Mom. I would have known him anywhere, because I had never stopped looking at his picture in my mind.

But today, he had looked right through me. He hadn't known me at all.

Apparently, I had been replaced by a guitar-playing six-year-old who could strum "Stairway to Heaven."

"You okay?" A voice cuts into my thoughts as I glide on autopilot through the dining room, ready to run another order back to the kitchen.

It takes me a moment to focus on a concerned-looking Nick sitting in his regular booth, his textbook spread out before him and a half-full glass of soda next to him.

"Couldn't be better," I say in my best chipper voice.

"You're doing a good job with the trays tonight," he says.

I force a quick smile at him. "Thanks. And thanks for your help last night." I turn for the kitchen.

"Wait," he says. I stop and notice that he looks a little nervous. "Listen. Do you want to go to a party with me tonight? It's just some friends of mine from school. I just want to stop by for a few hours."

The last thing I want to do is be around a group of college

students. I'm fully aware of how lucky I am to have gotten away with this incognito thing so far.

"I don't know . . . ," I begin. But Nick looks so cute and hopeful . . . and something inside me shifts.

"Please?" Nick says. "I mean, I know you said you just moved here. It will be a good way to meet people. And I hate showing up at parties alone."

I think about it for a moment and shrug. After all, what else am I going to do, sit home and sulk?

"Okay," I say, against my better judgment. "I'll go."

"You're awfully quiet," says Nick, glancing over at me. We've been in his Jeep for ten minutes, and I haven't said a word. I'm feeling really underdressed in the Rolling Stones tee, jeans and flip-flops that I arrived to work in that afternoon, but I didn't want to go back to my motel room. Nick still doesn't know I live at the good ol' Star Light next door. I have the feeling that if he did, it would lead to a whole slew of other questions that I just don't know how to answer.

"I've just had a long day," I say. "I'm sorry."

"It's cool," he says. "I just don't want you to feel like you have to come with me to this party if you don't want to. No pressure or anything."

"No," I say. I look at him and try to smile. "I want to go."

And I do. A little bit, anyhow. The more I think about it, the more intrigued I am. I've never *been* to a real party. Sure, there were birthday parties and stuff like that when I was a little kid, before I got famous. But I have the feeling this will be like one of those teenage parties I've seen on TV. And what could be more normal than going to a normal party with normal people? It's just one more step toward leaving Star Beck behind and becoming Amanda Mecham. Or Amanda Pepper. Or whoever I am.

"It's mostly some friends I went to high school with," Nick explains. "And some friends from college too. I won't know everyone there. But it'll be a cool group, I think."

"Well, thank you for inviting me," I say. Nick glances at me and smiles.

"I wanted my friends to meet you," he says.

I look at him in surprise.

"You told your friends about me?" I ask. He nods.

"You did? What did you say?"

"Just that you seem like a really cool girl," he says. He slows to a stop at a traffic light and turns his head to look straight at me. "And that I think I kind of like you."

My insides do a crazy somersault-backflip. Nick smiles at

me, winks one of his big brown eyes and then turns his attention back to the road.

We drive for another few minutes in silence, and I realize I'm finding it impossible to wipe the smile from my face.

I try not to think about the fact that our whole relationship so far is based on one big lie.

"This is Amanda." Nick introduces me to a group of guys and girls, all about his age, who are holding red plastic cups and who, to my relief, look as casual as I do. The girls are wearing jeans or denim skirts; most of the guys are in board shorts and tees. I feel myself start to relax a bit. Still, it's weird to hear myself introduced as Amanda. And my nerves are on edge, because I'm waiting for someone to realize who I really am.

"Hi." A small girl with short dark hair is the first to extend her hand to me. "I'm Anne."

Nick puts an arm around her.

"I've known Anne since we were kids," he says. I feel a weird little flicker of jealousy. It makes me feel funny to see him put his arm around her.

"I'm Ryan," says one of the guys, shaking my hand and

looking me up and down. "Dude," he says to Nick, "she's cute." Nick laughs, and I blush.

The others in the group introduce themselves too. Only one of them is giving me a funny look.

"I swear I've met you before," says Todd, a guy with bright blue eyes and blond hair tucked into an orange University of Florida Gators cap. "You look so familiar."

"I get that all the time," I say, averting my eyes and pushing my glasses farther up the bridge of my nose. My heart is pounding.

"Are you sure?" Todd asks. He's studying my face intently. "I could swear we've met. Do you go to UF?"

Nick jumps in and saves me. "Amanda just moved here from California."

"Weird," he says, shrugging. "You must look like someone I know or something."

A half hour later, the party is filling up. It's in the backyard of Ryan's parents' house. They're out of town this weekend, he explains, and he's home visiting from the University of Florida, where he's a freshman.

"Can I get you a beer?" he asks. "We've got three kegs out back. We're totally getting wasted tonight."

I shake my head. "I don't drink," I say. Ryan laughs and then whistles, loud and low. "A goody-goody!" he exclaims with a hoot.

He laughs, and I can feel my cheeks heat up. It's not like I object to drinking or anything, necessarily. I've just never really done it. My mom would obviously never let me have a beer. And since I can barely sneak Doritos past her, I seriously doubt I could be tossing back Budweisers all the time. But maybe Ryan's right. Maybe that *does* make me a goody-goody.

If only he knew that at this very moment, I am supposedly in rehab for alcohol addiction.

Nick appears out of nowhere, hands me a Coke and slips an arm around my shoulder.

"Hey, man, leave her alone," he says. Ryan grins and makes an *Ooh, I'm scared* face. Nick grins back and nudges him. "Dude, if she doesn't drink, she doesn't drink. It's cool. Lighten up. I'm just going to stick with Coke tonight too."

Everyone watches as he pops open a Coke and winks at me. I smile at him. It feels a little like he's come to my rescue. And I like it.

Thirty minutes later, it seems like everyone is drinking out of the kegs in the backyard except for Nick and me. The party's getting louder, more raucous and more crowded by the moment. People are doing keg stands, and there seems to be some kind of loud, off-key karaoke thing going on inside. There's a card game at the picnic tables, and people are starting to jump into the pool fully clothed. Nick excuses himself for a moment to go find the bathroom. I stand there for a minute, feeling conspicuously alone, until a girl walks over to me.

"You must be Amanda," she says. She has long brown hair and deep-set eyes, and she's staring at me. I glance from side to side.

"Yeah," I say. Who is this girl? She shifts her beer bottle from her right hand to her left.

"I'm Kallie," she says. Her eyes don't seem to be focusing on me quite right.

"Hi," I say, realizing that she's drunk.

"Are you with Nick?" she asks.

I nod.

"Did he tell you about me?" she asks.

I shake my head. I'm starting to wonder what this girl is up to. She doesn't look as friendly as I thought she did when she walked up. Actually, the look in her eyes is downright mean. I suddenly feel uneasy.

She laughs. "What am I going to do with him?" she says, her words slightly slurred. "He's probably leading you on and making you think he likes you," she adds.

I glance around for Nick.

"He's such a flirt," Kallie continues. She leans down so that our noses are almost touching. I can practically taste the beer on her breath. She holds a finger up in my face and jabs it at me. "But hands off, goody-goody," she says, her voice suddenly cold as ice. "He's my boyfriend. Don't you dare touch what's mine."

★

Chapter 14

I blink at her. "He's what?"

"My boyfriend," she says. A smug smile creeps across her face and she narrows her eyes. "Don't mess with him or you'll be sorry." Then she turns on her heel and wobbles away.

Nick returns a few minutes later with another Coke for me. He smiles, but I don't smile back.

"You okay?" he asks.

"I just met *Kallie*," I say. The smile falls from his face. "She says she's your girlfriend."

"Oh crap," Nick says. He looks guilty. Which probably means he *is*.

"Is she?" I ask. I try to remind myself that it's not like anything's ever happened between me and Nick. Maybe I don't have the right to be mad. Obviously, I just misread the signs and thought he liked me, when in reality, he had no interest at all. I feel like an idiot.

"It's a long story," Nick says with a sigh, not meeting my eye. "But I can explain," he adds.

"No need," I say, trying to sound cool and casual, like I don't care at all.

I turn away quickly and weave my way through the crowd, toward the kegs I know are in the back of the yard, near the fence. Despite myself, I hope he'll follow me to apologize or explain. I'm even more hurt when he doesn't. I really am a fool, I guess. *Fine*, I think, hating that there's an ache inside me now. What is it with everyone in my life always letting me down? *I've had enough for one day*.

Nick's friend Ryan is working the kegs when I get there. He laughs when he sees me and hands me a red plastic cup full of amber-colored beer.

"I knew you'd come over to the dark side!" he exclaims cheerfully as he thrusts the cup into my hand, sloshing some of it over the sides and down the legs of my jeans. "Bottoms up. Someone get this girl a shot!"

I glance behind me again to see if Nick has followed me, thinking that if maybe he has, if maybe he has an explanation, then maybe I shouldn't do this. But instead of Nick, I see a hand come out of the crowd with a Dixie cup of liquid.

"What is it?" I shout over the noise, taking the cup and sniffing it.

"Tequila!" says the guy attached to the hand. I look at him in confusion. He laughs and adds, "Just gulp it. You'll barely taste it."

What do I have to lose? It's not like there are paparazzi waiting in the bushes to capture this on film.

I gag immediately. Yuck! It tastes like rubbing alcohol and hurts as it slides down my throat. I start coughing as soon as I've swallowed. Ryan glances over and laughs.

"Woo-hoo!" he exclaims. "Drink some beer," he tells me. "It'll wash it down. It'll burn less."

I take a huge swig of beer. Then another. And another and another, until the beer—which tastes kind of like dirty socks but at least cools my throat—is gone.

"Fill 'er up!" Ryan grabs my empty cup, fills it up from the tap and hands it back to me. "You're my kind of girl after all!"

Thirty minutes later, I've had another tequila shot and

166

another beer, and I can't see straight anymore. I've almost lost my glasses three times because I keep forgetting that they're perched on my nose. I'm having trouble focusing, and suddenly, even though I'm mad at him, I wish I could find Nick in the crowd, just because he'd be a familiar face, and I'm feeling a little lost.

But he's nowhere to be seen. I'm crushed that not only does he have a girlfriend, but he's also apparently abandoned me at this party, which has swelled even bigger. There must be a hundred people in the yard, all of them jostling, most of them drunk, some of them yelling.

"Hey, new girl!" says a deep voice. I feel an arm around my shoulder, and as I turn, it takes me about thirty seconds to register that it's Nick's friend Todd.

"Where's Nick?" I yell over the din of the crowd.

"I think he's with Kallie!" he shouts back.

"His girlfriend?" I ask, trying not to sound bitter.

"Huh? Yeah!" Todd yells. "They've been going out for like six months. Hey, let's play a drinking game!"

I allow myself to be led, stumbling over plastic cups and empty bottles, toward the house. I follow Todd into the living room, where a group of twenty or so people is gathered around a big-screen TV.

"Karaoke?" I say as Todd leads me through the crowd.

"Drunk karaoke!" Todd clarifies. There's a girl singing

"Like a Virgin" off-key and attempting a little drunken dance near the TV. "Every time she messes up a word, everyone has to take a sip of their beer," Todd explains. "Let's play!"

I watch for a minute, and as the girl flubs a line and giggles, everyone laughs, raises their glasses and takes a big gulp of their beer.

"C'mon!" Todd urges. "Drink!" So I do.

I watch as "Like a Virgin" ends and another girl stands up.

"I'll sing!" she slurs.

The guy in the backward blue baseball cap running the karaoke machine punches in a few buttons, loads a new CD and yells out, "Oops! . . . I Did It Again!"

"You don't get to choose your own song?" I ask Todd as the music starts up again.

"No," he responds. "It's more fun when it's randomly chosen for you. That way, you screw up the lines more. And everyone gets wasted."

The girl messes up on the intro, and we all take big gulps of our beers. I'm feeling even woozier.

"I'll go get us some more beer!" Todd yells over the music. "Don't move!"

As soon as he's gone, I'm thinking about Nick again, wondering where he is and why he hasn't come to find me.

How could he not have mentioned Kallie to me? Did I totally misread everything?

I take another swig of my beer as the girl messes up the song again. Then it's over and the karaoke guy's eyes scan the crowd.

"You!" he says. It takes me a moment to realize he's pointing to me. "You're next!"

"Me?"

"What's your name?" he asks.

"A-Amanda," I stammer.

"Come on, A-Amanda!" he says back, obviously making fun of me. "We don't have all day!"

Everyone laughs. I just sit there. I can't get up and sing karaoke. What if someone recognizes me?

"A-man-da! A-man-da!" the people clustered around the TV start chanting. Nervously, I stand up and make my way to the front of the room. Everyone cheers. Karaoke Guy shuffles through his CDs, pops one in and grins at me.

"You're gonna sing Star Beck's 'You Don't Know Me,'" he announces. There are a few laughs in the crowd, and I can feel all the blood drain from my face. He pushes Play, and the familiar first chords of my song ring out.

"But I can't!" I exclaim as the karaoke machine plays the familiar intro. Everyone laughs.

"You *can't*?" asks Karaoke Guy, sounding amused. "Why?"

"Uh . . . I hate Star Beck!" I shout out the only thing I can think of.

"Star Beck's a hottie!" yells one guy.

"She's a slut!" yells another. "But I'd do her!" Everyone laughs. I feel sick.

"C'mon, Amanda!" Karaoke Guy says. "Everyone's gonna be pissed if you don't sing."

And so I do. Against all my better judgment, I stand up, wait for the intro to end and start belting out the words to my own song. And I realize immediately that I'm completely off-key, probably thanks to the liquor.

"*Don't stand so close,*" I begin. I clear my throat and my voice wobbles a bit. "*You can see my fears. Things aren't as perfect as they appear. You hold me close and wipe my tears.*" I stop for a minute for the instrumental break. The crowd has quieted a bit.

"She knows all the words!" exclaims one girl. I look at her guiltily and realize I haven't looked at the screen once.

"This sucks!" says another. "This is supposed to be a drinking game!"

"*But you don't know me,*" I continue singing. I feel my voice slip into key. "*You've never known me. Oh, oh, oh . . . Just leave me here!*"

I pause again for instrumentals. I look out at the crowd.

They're looking at me funny. I feel nauseous and shaky. Is it the alcohol or my nerves? I can't see straight. But with my own music playing behind me, I feel more at home than I have in a week. Suddenly, I'm back in my element. I close my eyes and launch into the chorus.

"*You don't know, you don't know, you don't know me!*" I sing, imagining Ben and the rest of the guys behind me, imagining that I'm onstage in some sold-out arena rather than at a party where I'm a stranger and the guy I like has a girlfriend and the father I lost doesn't know that I've found him. "*You say you do, you always say you do, but you never, never show me*," I continue. I'm in the moment, in my element. "*You're always telling lies to me, always in disguise with me. Open up your eyes to me and show me, show me . . . that you know me.*"

I crack open my eyes at the end of the chorus and am a little shocked to realize that the crowd gathered around the TV is now sitting in silence, staring at me.

"Dude, she's good," I hear one guy say. He burps and shakes his head.

"This sucks," whines a girl in a halter top. "I want to drink."

Crap, I think. My heart starts beating faster. *What am I doing?*

It's time for me to launch into the next verse. I glance at

the TV screen, clear my throat and begin singing deliberately off-key. I purposely flub the first line.

"I, uh . . . I love, love, love you," I sing.

"That's wrong!" yells one of the guys.

"Yeah!" yells another. "Drink, drink, drink!"

A sea of cups go bottom up, and I breathe a sigh of relief. I'm back in the moment now. I'm no longer onstage with Ben and the guys. I'm at a party full of drunken strangers in Florida. And if I don't sing off-key and screw up the words, someone's going to realize who I really am. What was I thinking?

"Amanda?" I hear a voice from the back of the room and see Nick standing in the doorway, staring at me. I'm so surprised that I completely forget the next lines.

"Nick," I say into the microphone.

"Sing!" yells a girl in the crowd. "What's wrong with you?"

I stare at Nick for a minute. I'm just about to say something to him when there's a bright flash of red and blue light outside and a man's voice comes over a bullhorn.

"Break it up!" says the loud voice, which seems to be coming from the front yard. "Party's over!"

Karaoke Guy stops the music. Everyone stands up and starts wildly dashing for doors, leaving their beers behind. I stare at the melee, bewildered.

"What's going on?" I ask.

Nick starts making his way toward me. I just stare at him. "Why are you just standing there? Come on! It's the cops!"

"What?" I ask. But Nick is already at my side. He scoops me up and carries me outside, going with the flow of bodies scrambling out of the yard through the back fence.

"Geez, Amanda," he says, setting me down and taking my hand once we're outside the fence. He pulls me along behind him as we run away from the house. "Are you trying to get arrested or something?"

He straps me into the passenger seat of his Jeep and pulls away from the curb.

"Are you okay to drive?" I ask as he pulls back onto Fourth Street.

"I was drinking soda all night," Nick says. He glances at me, and I can read annoyance in his eyes. "Unlike you, obviously."

"Yeah, well . . . ," I start to protest. Then I can't think of another single thing to say. The world is spinning. I don't feel good. I can't see straight. And it's been a really bad day. First my dad. Now Nick and Kallie. Part of me just wants to go home.

We drive in silence for a few minutes.

"I didn't know you drink," Nick says finally.

"I don't," I slur back. "Haven't you heard? I'm in rehab."

Nick looks at me funny, and I realize I shouldn't have said that. But he doesn't seem to know what I'm talking about. He shakes his head and turns his attention back to the road.

"Where do you live?" he asks.

"Why?" I ask suspiciously. He slows at a light and turns to look at me like I'm dense or something.

"So I can drop you off?" he says slowly.

"Oh," I say. "Right." I pause and shrug. "The motel. Next to your restaurant. The Star Light."

The light turns green. But Nick doesn't move. He's still looking at me.

"You live in a motel?" he asks.

"So?" I ask. I feel suddenly defensive.

"Why?"

There's a long honk behind us, and Nick turns his eyes back to road and presses down on the gas pedal.

"None of your business," I say, mustering as much haughtiness as I can. After all, I don't have to explain myself to some guy with a girlfriend. Nick starts to say something else, but then he stops and just shakes his head. We drive in silence for a few minutes, until we near the restaurant.

Nick puts his blinker on, pulls into the left lane and turns into the parking lot of the Star Light Motel.

He cuts the engine and we sit there in awkward silence for a moment. The world feels like it's spinning. I definitely shouldn't have had that last shot of tequila. Or that first shot of tequila. Or any of the beer, come to think of it.

"So why didn't you tell me you have a girlfriend?" I finally blurt out.

Nick looks startled. "Kallie?" he asks. "She's not my girlfriend."

"Whatever." I snort. "Todd said you've been dating for six months. And Kallie herself told me she's your girlfriend. Don't lie to me."

"I'm not," Nick says, shaking his head.

"I hate liars," I mumble. I cross my arms over my chest angrily. Or at least I try to. But somehow, my limbs are a little off, and I wind up whacking myself in the chest with my left hand instead. Nick looks like he's about to say something; then he just sighs.

"Look, Amanda," he says. "You're drunk. Let's say we talk about this tomorrow."

"Don't bother," I say. I struggle out of the car, stumbling a bit as I go but trying my best to maintain my balance. I slam the door behind me. "Everyone always betrays me anyhow," I say through the open window. Nick's eyebrows rise in apparent surprise. "I should have figured this would happen."

I march over to my door and fumble with the key for a

moment before the door opens. Despite everything, I'm still hoping that Nick will come after me, tell me I'm wrong and try to explain.

But instead, he just flashes his headlights at me once and drives away.

★

Chapter 15

I hate beer. And tequila.

I come to this conclusion the next morning. Or maybe one of the three times during the night that I have to drag myself out of bed to throw up.

But I'm pretty sure the hatred is fully in place when I finally wake up to the alarm clock at nine-thirty a.m. and realize that my head is throbbing so painfully I can't even see the alarm clock to shut it off.

"I. Am. Never. Drinking. Again," I moan into my pillow. All I can think about is getting some aspirin and drinking a gallon of water. I feel like I've been run over by a train.

No, being run over by a train would probably hurt less.

I take three aspirin and drink cup after cup of Star Light tap water. Then I sit back down on the bed. I have forty-five minutes before I have to be at D'Angelo's for the lunch shift.

I'm hoping Nick won't be there.

I'm mortified about last night. And also, I hate him a little bit for telling me he liked me, flirting with me and then turning out to have a girlfriend.

Jerk. Creep. Liar.

Too bad he's a cute jerk, creep and liar. That's the worst kind, I've realized.

I brush my teeth three times and still can't seem to rid my mouth of the taste of beer, tequila and vomit. Lovely. Then I wash my face, but the dark circles under my eyes don't seem to want to go away. Not even when I put my makeup on.

Did I mention I'm never drinking again?

Ugh.

I realize midway through getting dressed that tonight's open-mic night at the coffee bar downtown. The night I plan to tell my dad who I really am.

Then maybe I can get out of this crappy hotel, quit my job at D'Angelo's and never worry about seeing Nick again.

I flop back down on the bed and stare at the ceiling.

So far, normal isn't much fun. I'm pretty much out of money. I'm working a thankless job where customers are rude to me. I have the first real crush of my life and he turns out to be a jerky, creepy liar. And my own dad doesn't even recognize me.

I'm starting to think this was a mistake.

Impulsively, I dial *67 to do a call block on the phone; then I set the timer on my watch to go off after fifteen seconds. After all, that's how long it takes to do a phone trace on *Law & Order*. I dial and am surprised to realize how happy I suddenly feel when I hear a familiar voice on the other end.

"Hello?" Jesse says, then yawns.

"Jess, it's me," I say. "Star."

Silence.

"Star?" He sounds instantly awake. "Star, are you calling me from rehab?"

What? Even Jesse thinks I'm in rehab? He *knows* I don't drink. Well, I didn't drink before last night, anyhow.

"No!" I exclaim. "I'm not in rehab! I'm in St. Petersburg."

"Florida? What are you doing there?"

It's a good question. I'm beginning to wonder that myself.

"Uh, working in a restaurant called D'Angelo's."

"You ran away to work in a restaurant?" His voice is incredulous.

"Not exactly," I answer, hedging. "Look, I only have a second to talk. I just . . . I needed to hear a friendly voice. Things aren't going that well."

"What do you mean?" Jesse asks.

"I'm . . . I'm here to find my dad," I say. "I just met him yesterday. He doesn't even know me."

"What?" Jesse says. "Your dad? What are you talking about? Your dad disappeared when you were a baby."

"Well, apparently he didn't," I say quickly. "And anyhow, I just wanted a chance to be normal, you know? But I don't think I like it."

"Normal?" Jesse says. "What are you talking about? Why would you want to be *normal*?"

Like my mom, he says it like it's a bad word. The timer on my watch beeps.

"Jesse, I'm sorry. I have to go," I say. "I'll be home soon."

"Star! Don't hang up—"

I hang up.

At the restaurant I spot a familiar face.

"Hey, Amanda," she says as I approach her table reluctantly to get her drink order.

"Hi, Anne," I say. It's the dark-haired girl from last night, the one I met when Nick and I first arrived at the party. His longtime friend. One of the last people I want to see right now, thank you very much.

"Did you have a good time last night?" she asks.

"I guess," I say. I feel like an idiot. I'm sure she saw me drunk. How embarrassing. I renew my vow never to drink again. My head is still pounding. "What can I get you?" I ask politely.

"Look, Amanda?" Anne says. She reaches forward and puts her hand on my forearm. "Can I talk to you for a minute? About Nick?"

I look at her in surprise, then shake my head.

"I'm actually really busy right now," I say. The last thing I want to talk about now is Nick or anything having to do with Nick.

"No problem," Anne says. "I'll wait."

She orders a Coke and a pepperoni calzone, and she sits in my booth reading a book until the crowd has thinned out. At two p.m., she's still sitting there patiently, sipping her drink.

"Okay," I say reluctantly, materializing beside her table. "You wanted to talk to me?"

She nods. "Look, about last night . . . ," she says, her voice trailing off. "I heard you met Kallie."

I try not to make a face.

"Yeah," I say, trying to sound casual. "I didn't know Nick had a girlfriend."

Anne shakes her head.

"That's what I wanted to tell you," she says. "Kallie isn't his girlfriend. Not anymore, anyhow. They dated for six months. Then she cheated on him with some football player guy at her school."

I look at Anne skeptically.

"But everyone at the party last night seemed to think they were still together," I say. "And Kallie said so herself."

"Kallie's a liar," Anne says. The vehemence in her voice surprises me. "She totally regrets cheating on him. The new guy dumped her like a week later and started dating some cheerleader. Kallie was totally embarrassed. She's been trying to get Nick back ever since. But he doesn't want anything to do with her. I think he feels really betrayed."

"I know how that feels," I mutter.

"Nick didn't want to embarrass her," Anne continues. "The people at the party last night, most of them don't even know Nick that well, so it's not like he's going to go around and tell all of them that Kallie cheated on him. I don't think he cares much what they think. So that's why some of them still think Nick and Kallie are together."

I digest this for a minute.

"Why are you telling me all this?" I ask.

Anne shrugs.

"I think Nick really likes you," she says. "I just didn't want Kallie, of all people, to screw things up."

Nick's waiting outside the restaurant when I finish my shift at four.

"I hear Anne came to see you," he says when I walk out. I look at him for a moment and nod. "I'm sorry," he mutters. "I didn't ask her to."

"She told me about Kallie," I say. Nick nods. He sits down on the curb, and I join him.

"I know," he says after a moment. "I'm sorry I didn't explain last night. I had a long talk with her about how she needs to leave me alone and stop trying to get me back. That's why I was gone so long. When I was done, I couldn't find you."

"I thought you'd left with her or something," I say.

"I wouldn't have done that."

"Oh." I hesitate for a moment and add, "Look, I'm sorry too. I never drink. I know I acted like an idiot last night."

Nick shakes his head.

"Yeah, well," he says. "I have to say that you're not exactly at your most attractive at the keg." I look at him for a minute and realize he's fighting back a grin. I laugh and playfully punch him in the arm.

"Thanks a lot," I say.

There's a moment of silence between us.

"Can I ask you something?" Nick blurts out suddenly. "Last night, you had me drop you off at the Star Light," he says, nodding across the parking lot at the chipped and peeling motel. "Do you really *live* there?"

"Yes," I say simply.

"Why?" he asks.

Instead of answering, I say, "Would you walk me home?"

Nick nods and we walk in silence across the parking lot to the motel. I unlock the door to room 112, and Nick follows me inside. I watch as he takes everything in. His eyes rove from the faded, peeling carpet to the broken dresser to the bed that sags in the middle to the dirty walls, finally alighting on the Raid canister sitting on the nightstand.

"You have bugs?"

"A whole family of roaches," I say, rolling my eyes. "I'm getting used to them."

"You are?" Nick asks.

I think for a minute, then laugh. "No, actually, I'm not," I admit. "I can hardly sleep. I hate them."

We stand there for a moment. Then Nick puts both of his hands on my shoulders and looks down at me

"Really. Why are you staying in this place?" he asks slowly. I look up at him and can only muster a shrug. He stares at me for a minute, then shakes his head and averts his eyes. "I'm sorry," he mumbles. "It's not my business."

"No," I say quickly. "Don't say that. I appreciate ... I appreciate that you care."

Nick looks at me for a moment, then removes his hands from my shoulders and sits down on the edge of my bed. I do the same, leaving a foot of space between us. He seems to be thinking about something. Finally, he speaks.

"Look, Amanda, it's just that you're kind of mysterious," he begins, looking at the floor.

"I'm sorry. I—"

"Kallie was all mysterious for a couple of months. I thought it was kind of cute at the time. But I realized later it was because she was lying about stuff. And cheating on me. So I guess I'm kinda weird now about mysteriousness and avoiding questions and stuff."

"I'm sorry," I repeat.

"It's not like you have to tell me anything you don't want to," Nick continues. "It's just . . . I haven't really liked anyone since Kallie. Then I saw you at the restaurant, and, well, you spilled those drinks on me, and we talked for a minute, and I actually felt something I hadn't felt in a while."

"Ice?" I kid him, trying to break the seriousness that seems to have settled over us. It's making me uncomfortable. Nick laughs.

"And sticky soda," he says with a half grin. Then he looks at me seriously. "What I mean is, I like you." He pauses and looks nervously at me. "Too much?" he asks.

"No," I say with a laugh. I can feel myself blushing. This might be the first time in my whole life someone has simply liked me for *me*.

"Well, anyhow, I thought you seemed really nice," he says. "But I'm not a big fan of secrets."

"But I'm not trying to hide another guy or anything," I say. "I swear."

He gives me another half grin. "Well, that's good."

We sit in silence for a minute. "Anyhow, you don't have to tell me anything you don't want to. I just wanted you to know where I'm coming from."

I feel bad. I feel terrible. I want to tell him the truth. But I know I can't.

After a moment, Nick reaches over and folds his hand around mine. I look down at our intertwined fingers, then back up at him. He smiles at me.

"I have to go to an open-mic night downtown tonight at nine," I hear myself blurt out before I can stop. Sheesh, apparently Nick's holding my hand made all common sense fly out the window. But I've said it. I might as well dig myself deeper into the hole. "Will you come with me?" I ask.

He grins. "What, you want to sing more Star Beck songs?" he asks. I freeze in horror for a moment, wondering how on earth he's suddenly figured out who I am. Then I realize that all he's talking about is my karaoke nightmare last night.

"Uh, yeah, that's it," I say with a shaky laugh. "You got me. I can't get enough of that Star Beck."

Nick laughs.

"Really, though," he says. "Why do you have to go to this open-mic thing?"

I think for a minute about telling him that my long-lost father is the guy who runs the show. I almost say it. But somehow, I can't. My own father hasn't even acknowledged me yet. How can I tell Nick about him? And how could I possibly tell him that without having to explain everything else too?

"Um, well, I sing and play the guitar," I say instead, avoiding his gaze. "I was thinking about maybe taking some lessons."

I expect him to react like I've said something ridiculous, because it sounds really silly to me. But instead, he smiles and squeezes my hand.

"See, now you're telling me something about yourself,

Miss Mysterious," he says with a smile. "It wasn't that bad, was it? And yes, I would love to come and hear you play the guitar."

"Really?" I ask.

"Really. How about I pick you up at eight-thirty?"

"Okay," I agree. I suddenly realize that this could be considered a date. Have I actually made a real date?

Nick lets go of my hand. "I should go," he says, standing up from the bed. He seems suddenly nervous. I stand up too and nod.

"Okay," I say. We walk toward the door in silence.

"Okay," Nick echoes. We stand by the doorway for a moment, just looking at each other. Then Nick takes a step closer. I feel like the world is moving in slow motion as I look up at him, just inches away from me. He puts his left hand gently behind my head and sort of caresses my scalp under my hair for a moment. Then he dips his face toward mine, closes his eyes and kisses me softly on the lips.

Oh my God. He tastes like Coke and pizza and boy and every other good thing I can think of. He's perfect.

I close my eyes too and kiss him back.

It's amazing.

Although I've fake-kissed several guys, everything about Nick feels different. His lips are soft, and he presses them against mine gently, sweetly, and I know that this, finally, is what it's supposed to feel like.

He leaves, eventually, kissing me good-bye once more on the top of my head and promising to see me in a few hours.

And for a long time after he's gone, I can still feel the tingle of his lips against mine.

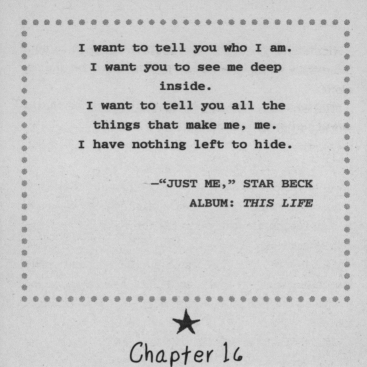

I want to tell you who I am.
I want you to see me deep
inside.
I want to tell you all the
things that make me, me.
I have nothing left to hide.

—"JUST ME," STAR BECK
ALBUM: *THIS LIFE*

Chapter 16

"Welcome to open-mic night at Muggs, sponsored by Mecham's Music," says my father in a booming voice as he steps onto the small stage at the downtown coffeehouse. He's dressed in dark jeans and a pale blue collared shirt. "As most of you know, I'm Pete Mecham, the owner of Mecham's Music."

Nick takes my hand. I'm glad he's here. His warm fingers laced through mine make me feel like I'm not quite so alone.

"Those of you who have been here before know how this works," my father continues. "But I see a few new faces, so I'll explain it quickly. For everyone who has signed up, you'll have a chance to perform one song."

My father calls a name into the mic, and a college-age guy with a plaid shirt and faded jeans shuffles to the stage, accepts the guitar my father hands him and starts to play a Nickelback song.

"This is cool," Nick says, leaning in and speaking softly into my ear as the guy belts out "Photograph." I can feel his breath on me, and a tingle runs down my spine. "Thanks for inviting me."

"Thanks for coming," I whisper back. When the Nickelback guy has finished, my father calls up a blond girl named Ashley, who comes to the stage, sits down at the piano and starts to slowly pick out a Jewel tune on the keyboard. Everyone claps when she's done. She smiles, looks relieved and slinks back to her table, where she's sitting with an older woman.

My father thanks Ashley for her "terrific rendition of one of Jewel's most popular songs," then looks at a notecard and says, "Well, it appears we have a new musician joining us tonight. I'd like to welcome to the stage . . . Amanda Pepper."

Nick nudges me.

"But I didn't—" I begin, panicked.

"You said you wanted to play," Nick says with a grin. "So I put your name on the list." He clearly thinks he's done something nice for me, but playing is the *last* thing I want to do. What if I sound too much like myself? What if someone recognizes me? I'd prefer to just blend into the woodwork and watch my dad from afar.

"Do we have an Amanda Pepper here?" my father asks from the stage, squinting into the small audience.

I look from Nick to my dad and then back at Nick again.

"You don't have to if you don't want to," Nick whispers. He looks worried. "I just thought you said you wanted to play."

I think for a second and then nod. "Yeah. Okay." I make my way up to the stage, where my father smiles at me. There's a smattering of polite applause.

"Hi there," my father says as I step onto the stage. "I know you. You're the girl from the store yesterday."

I nod, sad that the glint of recognition in his eye reaches back just thirty-six hours instead of sixteen years.

"Guitar, right?" he says, already handing me the one the college guy played the Nickelback song on. I take a deep breath and focus on tuning it for a moment while he steps down. I feel naked and exposed as I stand on the tiny stage in this small room, about to play to probably the smallest audience I've ever performed for. I settle onto a stool, adjust the microphone and think about what I'll play.

"Hello," I say nervously into the mic, my voice cracking oddly as I speak. I clear my throat. "I'm going to play a song I wrote called 'Remember Me.'" I glance out at Nick and see him beaming at me proudly. I search the room for my father and my heart sinks when I see him at the coffee counter, his back to me, not paying me the slightest bit of attention. I take a deep breath, strum a few chords and begin the song.

"I can't believe I've lost you," I sing. *"I can't believe you're gone."* I strum softly along, getting lost in one of my favorite songs, a song I wrote last year that Mom never lets me play. It's the first time I've ever played a song I've written for an audience. Thankfully for the sake of staying incognito, it doesn't sound anything like a typical Star Beck song.

I look out at the room as I continue singing. Nick's mouth is slightly open, and my father, who has turned around from the coffee bar, is staring at me. I don't think I've blown my cover. Still, I'm not sure why they're looking at me so intently. I take a breath and launch into the chorus, my voice rising an octave.

"You were my world, my life, my soul," I continue. *"Now you've been away for far too long."*

I close my eyes and imagine for a moment that my father is listening to me, recognizing me, realizing that the words, the notes, the melodies are all for him. But when I open my eyes again and look at him, I know in an instant that all he's seeing is a girl who's pretty good at the guitar. There's no recognition on his face, no glint in his eyes, no hint of affection on his features.

Nick's face is a different story. He's staring at me, his mouth hanging open, as if he's seeing me for the first time.

By the time I'm playing through the chorus for the last time, my loneliness feels painfully raw.

"You've been away for far too long," I conclude.

As I strum the last chord and set the guitar down, back in its stand, I look out at the audience and feel the carpet of comfort yanked out from under me. They're all staring at me, and I feel suddenly embarrassed. They hated me. They thought my song was terrible. Mom was right after all; I shouldn't even be attempting my own music.

But then a funny thing happens. One of the fifty-something bald men in the back starts clapping and then everyone joins in, and it doesn't stop. It's loud, thundering applause, applause that seems too big to come from this small crowd. I look out at them in shock. They're smiling, cheering, and a guy in the back is even making whooping sounds and pumping his fist in the air.

I can hardly believe it. They liked *me*. Not Star Beck. Not the pop star–molded, perfectly dressed, perfectly choreographed Star Beck. But me. Just me and a guitar.

Me.

I blush, mutter a nervous "Thank you" into the mic and step down from the stage. I make my way back to the table I'm sharing with Nick and slide into my seat.

"That was amazing," he says slowly.

"It was no big deal," I mumble, but secretly, I'm thrilled.

"Wow," says my father into the mic as he steps onto the stage. "I think we can all agree that was a pretty incredible performance. Let's hear it again for"—he pauses and consults his sheet of paper—"Amanda Pepper!" The crowd claps and cheers again, and my father beams at me.

As my father calls up the next performer, Nick squeezes my hand. But even with him holding my hand tightly, I feel very lost and alone.

"I have a surprise for you," Nick says later that night as we pull into the parking lot of the Star Light Motel.

"You do?" I smile.

Nick looks at me for a long moment. "I told my mom and dad about where you were staying."

I can feel the smile melt from my face. "You did?" I didn't want anyone else to know.

Nick nods. "They were as horrified as I was."

"It's not that bad," I say defensively.

"It's pretty bad," Nick says.

I make a face. "Fine, so it's awful. But I'll be okay. Anyhow, it's not like I have anywhere else to go right now."

"That's where you're wrong." He turns to me. "You know how I said I was staying in the little apartment above the restaurant?"

I nod, and Nick continues.

"Well, I talked to my mom and dad, and they said it's fine if you move in there for a little while."

I can feel the blood drain from my face. "What? Nick, I barely know you. I can't live with you! I can't even believe your mom and dad would be okay with that!"

Nick laughs. "No!" he exclaims. "I mean, I moved my stuff home to my parents' house this afternoon. I'll stay with them for a few weeks. It's no big deal. The apartment above the restaurant is so tiny you can barely turn around in it, but at least it's not infested with roaches. And the sheets have actually been washed this decade."

"Nick!" I exclaim. I'm floored. "I can't take your apartment!"

"Sure you can," he says. "And you'd better. Because I know I'm not going to be able to sleep at night thinking of you being in this dirty motel."

"I have Raid," I say weakly. "I'll be fine. Really."

"I'm not discussing it further," he says firmly. "Go pack up. I'll help you move your stuff."

I open my mouth to protest again, but Nick shushes me.

"Seriously, Amanda," he says. "There's no way I'm letting you stay here."

"Nick, I don't even know what to say. I'll give your parents everything I make at the restaurant, but I don't really think I can pay them much rent right now . . . ," I begin. I can feel my cheeks flush in embarrassment. Nick shakes his head.

"Amanda, no one expects you to pay for the apartment. We all agreed that you couldn't keep living here. Now stop worrying and start packing, okay?"

I can feel tears prick the back of my eyes. I think this is the first time someone has done something for me without expecting something in return. I don't even know how to react.

"Nick, I swear, I will pay you and your parents back someday," I say. I look into his eyes. "I swear to God."

Nick laughs. "It's really no big deal," he says. "Don't tell anyone, but it's kinda nice to be back at my parents' place, for a little while, anyhow. My mom makes way better lasagna than they make at the restaurant. And she does my laundry for me. Now stop worrying. Let's go get your stuff."

Not surprisingly, considering I barely have anything with me, it only takes a few minutes to pack.

"You sure travel light," Nick says, looking at me a little funny after he's zipped up my duffel. He swings the bag over his shoulder.

"Yeah," I say noncommittally, hoping he won't ask me to explain. Thankfully, he doesn't.

The room above the restaurant, which is accessible through a private stairway that opens to the back parking lot, is tiny, but I feel instantly at home. It clearly wasn't designed to be an apartment; even with the twin bed pushed against the wall, it's barely big enough to move around in, and the teeny adjoining bathroom has only a shower and a sink.

"You have to use the toilet downstairs," Nick says a bit sheepishly. "Sorry."

"It's fine," I say, and I mean it. "Actually, it's perfect."

And it is. For the first time, I'm somewhere that feels

like a home. The bed is covered with a quilt that looks homemade, there's a tiny bedside table with a reading lamp and a few novels, and there are even a few photos of Italy pinned to the wall. Best of all, there's no sign of roaches.

"Nick, I don't even know how to thank you," I whisper.

"It's thanks enough to not have to worry about you being in that awful place next door," he says dismissively. He hands me the key to the outside door. "Now are you going to unpack or what?"

Ten minutes later, Nick and I sit down side by side on the edge of the twin bed.

"You know, I meant to tell you how amazing you were tonight," he says. "At the open-mic night, I mean. You're an unbelievable singer."

"Thanks." His words make me feel good, but I'm unsettled. Singing in front of my dad—and *still* not having him recognize me—has made me feel emptier than I expected. Even the high of being appreciated by an audience who didn't realize I'm Star Beck isn't enough to bring me back.

"I mean, really," Nick continues, shooting me a glance that looks almost nervous. "You blew everyone away."

"Thanks," I say again.

"You should think about doing that professionally," he says helpfully. This makes me laugh. I can't help it.

"Yeah?" I say. "Maybe I will someday."

"Listen, is something bothering you?" Nick asks. "You've been sort of quiet. Is it the apartment? Or did I do something?"

"No," I say. "I really appreciate the apartment. And it's not you."

"Then what is it?" Nick says. "You can talk to me if something's wrong, you know."

I think about it for a minute. I don't know what to say. I'm not sure I'm ready for the truth. But the longer I'm here, away from the world I know, the lonelier I feel. It would be nice to tell someone my story. At least part of it.

"Nick, I came here to find my dad," I finally say. Nick looks surprised, but he nods, waiting for me to go on. I study his face for a moment then continue. "Well, I found him. He was the emcee of the open-mic night tonight." Nick just stares at me for a moment.

"That Mecham's Music guy?" he asks.

"Yes," I say simply.

"But he didn't act like he was your dad," Nick says slowly.

"He doesn't recognize me," I say. I look at Nick miserably. "I've seen him twice since I got here, and he doesn't know me."

"Wait, wait," Nick says, looking confused. "I don't understand."

For a moment, I look at my lap and think about what to say. I glance back up at Nick.

"I thought for a long time that my father walked out on my mom and me when I was three years old. Then, last week, someone gave me a letter that he'd written to me. I confronted my mom about it and found out he'd been writing to me once a month for the last six years."

Nick stares at me in silence for a moment.

"What?" he finally asks incredulously. "And your mom was keeping the letters from you?"

I nod.

"That's terrible!" he exclaims.

"I just can't believe he doesn't recognize me," I confess. "I mean, isn't a parent supposed to be able to pick his child out of a crowd? Isn't that the way it's supposed to work?"

"Well, obviously you look really different now than when you were three."

"But he's seen me since then," I say without thinking about it. "My picture, at least. All the time."

"What do you mean?" Nick asks. I look at him quickly. Oops. I almost slipped.

"Never mind," I say. I don't know what I was looking for, exactly. Comfort? Advice? But Nick is just sitting there. I feel stupid. Then he takes a deep breath and looks resolutely at me.

"You have to tell him," he says.

"What?"

"You have to tell him who you are."

"But how am I going to do that?" I protest. "What, just walk in and go, 'Hi, Dad, remember me?'"

"It's what you came here for, isn't it?" Nick asks.

I shrug. "I guess so."

"Then you have to do it," he says. "Or you'll regret it. He's your dad, Amanda. And if he's been writing to you for the last six years, he still loves you. He'll *want* to meet you."

"I guess you're right." After all, what point is there in this whole thing if I don't approach my dad and tell him who I am?

"Amanda?" Nick asks after a minute. "What did you mean a minute ago when you said your dad had seen you all the time in pictures since you were a kid?"

I don't know what to tell him.

"Was your mom sending him pictures or something?"

I hesitate. I could say yes and avoid the whole issue. But I realize I don't want to.

"No," I say slowly. "He could have seen me anytime. On TV. In magazines. Wherever."

"What?" Nick asks, obviously thoroughly confused.

"This isn't what I usually look like," I explain, watching Nick's face. There's still no glint of recognition. "I had to change my look to come here or people would have recognized me."

"Who?" he asks, looking concerned and confused. "Who would have recognized you?"

I think about stopping here. I think about smiling and saying I was just kidding. After all, I've done such a good job of blending in. I've been so good about being the *real* me by taking on a fake identity. I almost don't want to give it up.

But I *want* Nick to know who I am. I don't know why. It just feels important.

"Everyone," I finally say. "Nick. Imagine me without the glasses." I take off my glasses and look at him. He's still staring at me in confusion.

"Imagine me with more makeup on."

Still nothing.

"Imagine me with red hair," I say. He looks at me blankly.

"Long, curly red hair," I prompt, waiting for the spark of recognition.

Instead, he's still just staring at me. "I really don't know what you're talking about," he says finally. "I think you're pretty the way you are, Amanda."

"My name isn't Amanda," I say softly. "Not anymore."

"What?"

"Nick," I say. "I'm Star Beck."

You don't see me crying,
do ya?
You don't see me walking away.
I'm here now.
I'm here now.
I'm here to stay, to stay,
to stay (hey, hey).

—"I'M HERE," STAR BECK
ALBUM: *STAR LIGHT*

★

Chapter 17

*I*t seems like time has stopped while I wait for Nick to respond. He just stares at me for what feels like an eternity. My mouth feels dry, and my heart is pounding as I wait for him to say something. I have no idea how he's going to react, and I'm beginning to think I shouldn't have opened my big mouth. Everything was going just fine. Why did I have to go and screw it all up?

"You're Star Beck," Nick says flatly. I can't tell what he's thinking.

I nod.

"The pop star," Nick says, as if there could be another Star Beck I'm talking about.

"That's me," I say.

"This doesn't make any sense," he says finally.

"What do you mean?" I ask, my voice tentative.

"I mean . . . ," Nick's voice trails off. "If you're really Star Beck, what are you doing here?"

"Looking for my dad," I say, disturbed that he doesn't seem to believe me. "I told you the truth about that. It's a long story, but he and my mom broke up when I was a kid, and she's been keeping him from me ever since. I just found out."

Nick just stares at me for another moment, and I feel sad. I just want him to reach over and embrace me and say something comforting like *I understand, and it's okay that you lied about who you are. Don't worry about your dad; I'm sure he's never stopped loving you.*

Instead, he says, "You don't look like Star Beck." Then he adds, "Not that I'm a big fan or anything."

I reach for my wallet. I dig through until I emerge with my California state driver's license.

"Here's proof if you need it," I say, handing him the

license. He looks at me for a moment; then he takes the license and looks down at it.

"It says Amanda Star Beckendale," he says, studying it with a confused look on his face. "So your name *is* Amanda."

"Yeah," I say. "But I use my middle name as my stage name. If you don't believe it's me, just Google me online. It's on, like, a million sites that that's my real name."

Nick hands back my license. "No," he says finally. He sighs and looks away. "I believe you. I just . . ." His voice trails off and he shakes his head. "I just don't know what to say."

"You don't *have* to say anything." I reach over and put my hand on his. "I just wanted you to know. I wanted to be honest with you. I—I think I really just need a friend right now."

Nick slowly pulls his hand away.

"Amanda . . . or Star . . . or whoever you are," he begins, a troubled look on his face. "Geez, I don't even know what to call you. I just . . ." He pauses again. "This is just a lot to deal with, you know?"

"Why?" I ask, feeling a sort of desperation set in. "I'm still the same person. I mean, you *know* me."

"No, I don't," Nick says. He stands up to leave. "I know a klutzy waitress named Amanda Pepper. But this . . . this makes everything really confusing. I just need to think about things for a little while."

"What is there to think about?" I ask, hating how needy my voice suddenly sounds.

"It's just a lot to absorb," Nick says. He stands up to leave. "I'm sorry. I know you want me to say something different. But I really don't know what to say right now.

"I'm sorry," he says softly on his way out. I nod, afraid that if I speak, I'll cry. "Don't worry," he adds, like an afterthought. "I won't tell anyone. Your secret's safe."

"Thanks," I say. I appreciate it. But I hate that I have this secret at all. I hate that I can't just be me. Before I can say that, Nick, the one person in the world who saw me for what I am inside rather than for all my Grammys and hits and hype, is gone.

I walk up to my father's store the next morning after a mostly sleepless night. I tossed and turned and hoped that Nick would come back, but he never did. Somewhere over the course of the night I decided to do my best to just let him go. I didn't come to St. Petersburg for him; I came here to find my dad. And that's what I have to focus on.

I spot him immediately, in the guitar room, his back to

me. He's restringing a guitar. The store has just opened, and I'm the first customer here. I don't see another sales-person. We seem to be alone.

I take a deep breath, stride across the room and stop a foot away from him.

"Hi," I say. He turns around, looks at me for a moment and smiles pleasantly.

"Well, hello there," he says brightly. "Amanda Pepper, right? You were fantastic last night. Have you come to sign up for lessons?"

"No," I say softly. "I'm not here for lessons."

He looks pained.

"Now, now, don't be hasty," he says right away. "Your technique is great. But I can definitely work with you to improve your chord sequences. And the pitch of your voice."

I look at him for a moment, slightly caught off guard. What's wrong with the pitch of my voice?

"No," I say after a moment. "That's not what I'm here to talk about."

He studies my face for a moment. I will him to realize who I am. I wait for his face to light up in recognition. But it doesn't happen.

"What do you mean?" he finally asks. He stops restring-ing the guitar and just stands there holding it.

"I'm here to meet you," I say.

"Me?" he asks.

"Dad," I say softly. "I'm your daughter. Amanda. Amanda Star Beckendale-Mecham."

"Oh my God," he says. Then he promptly drops the guitar, sending it clattering to the floors in a symphony of mashed strings.

"Star, honey, I thought I'd never get to see you again," my father says, staring intently at me.

We're in his office in the back of the store. He's behind his desk, and I'm in an uncomfortable, hard-backed chair facing him. It feels wrong somehow, oddly formal. I want him to hug me and welcome me home. But maybe that's crazily unrealistic. Maybe that just happens in made-for-TV movies. Instead, he's just staring at me across a wide, cluttered desk.

"I didn't know you were trying to get in touch with me," I explain, hoping he can tell how much I regret not knowing. "I didn't get any of your letters. Until last week."

"You didn't get them?" he asks. I shake my head as he mutters a bunch of unprintable things about my mom. "Did she say why?"

I shrug. I don't want to get into Mom's motives. Not now.

My father shakes his head slowly and stares at me some more.

"You don't look like I thought you would," he says. "I mean, you look different on TV and in all the magazines."

"Well," I say, "I cut and dyed my hair. And I'm wearing glasses. I didn't want people to recognize me. I didn't want to come here as Star Beck. I wanted to just be here as your daughter. Without the media and stuff."

"My God," he says again, shaking his head as he continues to stare. I think he's taking it all in, and I feel nervous, waiting to see how he reacts. "I heard you were in rehab," he says.

I roll my eyes. "I've never been in rehab," I say.

He studies me intently. "I just can't believe you're here. Star Beck. Here. In my office."

I look at him strangely. It almost sounds like he's impressed to have a pop star in his presence, instead of impressed to have his daughter home at last.

"You used to call me Amanda," I remind him. "When I was little. Do you remember?"

"Sure!" he says. "I used to take you to the playground. You used to love to slide down the twisty slide. Remember?"

"You were always there to catch me," I say in a small voice.

"Always," he says. He stares at me for a minute more, then shakes his head again. "Star—Amanda, I mean—I want you to meet my wife and daughter. I mean, they're your family too. I want you to know your sister."

"My sister," I echo. It's a weird thought. I've been an only child all my life. Or at least I thought I was. How strange to know there's another child out there who's my own flesh and blood. Half, anyhow.

He picks up a framed photo from his desk and holds it out to me. The little girl in the picture has wispy blond hair and a crooked smile with a missing front tooth. I've never seen her before. But she looks familiar. She looks like me. She has the same stormy green eyes my dad and I have. "Her name's Alison. She's in kindergarten."

I feel sad as I hand the photo back to him. Did he used to hand people my picture when I was a little girl? Or did he forget about me as soon as he was gone? The thought hurts.

"She's really cute," I say, knowing it's crazy to be jealous of this innocent little girl. But she has the childhood I never got to have. A normal home with her mom and dad. *My* dad.

"So how about it?" my father asks. "Can you come over for dinner tonight? At, say, six? I'll call Lynda—that's my wife—and tell her. Can you?"

"Yes," I say instantly. "Of course. I'd love to."

He jots down his address for me. I don't tell him I already

have it, that I've already been there, standing outside imagining what my life would be like if I lived there with him. Then he gets up and walks me toward the door. I'm a little surprised our meeting is over. I had somehow envisioned him taking the whole rest of the day off to talk to me, to catch up with me, maybe even to take a walk in a park or playground to reminisce. But I guess that was unrealistic.

"Star," my father says. "I can't tell you how happy I am to see you again."

"Me too," I say. My heart pounds as he approaches me. We're about to hug for the first time in thirteen years. *I'm about to hug my father. My own dad.* I never thought this day would come.

"Nice to see you," my father says, extending his hand. I stare at it for a moment, not quite sure what to do. A handshake? He's going to shake my hand? I feel suddenly breathless. I reach a trembling hand out and slip it into his. His big hand wraps around my little one, and he pumps it up and down enthusiastically. "I'll see you tonight for dinner."

"Okay," I say, trying to keep the uninvited tremor out of my voice. I allow myself to be led back into the main room and then out through the front door. I turn back and stare once I'm outside. But he's already disappeared back into the depths of the store.

"Star!" exclaims the blond woman who answers the door at my father's house that night. She's wearing a black cocktail dress and a string of ivory pearls around her neck. Her hair's up in a twist. She looks awfully fancy for a family dinner. "I'm your father's wife, Lynda. What an honor to have you here!"

My stepmother, I think. *Stepmom.*

"It's nice to be here," I respond as I follow her into the house, drinking in every detail as I go. The house is spotless. The sofas in the living room look faded as Lynda leads me through to the dining room, and the TV they face is small and at least a decade old. But everything looks freshly vacuumed and dusted.

"We had a cleaning service come in today and freshen the place up," Lynda says proudly, as if reading my mind. "We wanted everything to be perfect for you."

"You didn't have to do that," I say in surprise.

"Oh no, Peter insisted," she says. "Your dad, I mean."

It sounds weird to hear her say that. I force a smile and follow her into the dining room. Her words keep replaying in my head. *Your dad. Your dad. Your dad.*

"Please, Star, have a seat," Lynda says, leading me over to the dining room table. It has already been set—with nice, white china and sparkling glasses.

"Do you use china every night?" I ask, imagining my father having fancy dinners every time he comes home from work.

"Oh no," Lynda laughs. "This is our special-occasion china. Now have a seat, dear. I'll go get Alison and Peter—er, your dad."

I sit down awkwardly in a high-backed dining room chair and wait. I'm feeling uneasy. I didn't want my dad and his wife to go to any trouble. I feel weird enough already without them making this such a big production. But maybe it means my father is just eager to get back into my life.

I wish for a moment that I had someone familiar here with me. Ben, maybe. Or Jesse. Or even Nick, although that doesn't seem like much of a possibility. I resolve to try to forget about him. For now, anyhow.

"Star!" my father's voice booms. I turn to see him entering the dining room. He's wearing a pale blue shirt and a navy blue tie with gray pants. His arms are open wide, and he's smiling as he approaches. Instinctively, I stand up to greet him. This time, he wraps me in a warm hug. I feel my heart melt, and I hug back, surprised by the familiarity of it all. I'm taken aback to realize how clearly I remember being hugged by him all of a sudden.

"Hi," I say as we pull away. "Your house is really nice."

"Thank you." My father beams. "We had a cleaning service come today. Nothing but the best for you."

"Star?" I hear Lynda reenter the room behind us. I turn, and my eyes instantly settle on the little girl she has with her. Alison is staring at me with the same wide green eyes I have, looking uncomfortable in a frilly pale pink party dress that's a little too small for her. "This is our daughter, Alison," she says.

"Hi," I say softly, unable to take my eyes off her. I feel like the wind has been knocked out of me.

"Hi," she says, staring right back at me. I squat down next to her and look her in the eye.

"I'm Star," I say. "But you can call me Amanda if you want. That's my real name."

"So why do you say your name is Star if it's not your real name?" she asks suspiciously. I smile.

"It's just what everyone calls me," I say. I glance up at my father and Lynda, both of whom are smiling. I look back at Alison.

"Mommy says you're that famous singer," she says. "The one who sings 'Fight Fire with Fire.'"

"Yes," I say. "I am."

"You don't look like her," she says.

My father nudges Alison. "Isn't there something you wanted to say to Star?" he asks. Alison looks confused for a moment, then her face lights up.

"Oh yeah," she says. "Would you be my sister?" she asks.

I can feel tears fill my eyes. For a moment, I can't speak. There's a lump in my throat. I gulp it back and smile.

"I'd love to be," I say.

But as we all sit down to eat, I can't silence the little voice in the back of my head that tells me her words sounded strangely rehearsed.

I feel underdressed in my gray Amy Tangerine tee, jeans and sneakers. It didn't occur to me that my dad and his family would be dressed up like they're on their way to church or something.

First, we eat tomato bisque.

"My mother's recipe," Lynda explains nervously as she sets a bowl down in front of me. I tell her it's delicious. Then comes a small salad, then prime rib, mashed potatoes and asparagus. Everything's good. But I feel strange. Every time I look up, all three of them are staring at me. My father and Lynda quickly avert their eyes each time. But Alison, who obviously isn't quite as well versed in the rules of politeness, just continues to stare.

"Mommy and Daddy never told me I had a sister," Alison announces, midway through her prime rib. I try not to let the words sting. After all, why *would* my father have said anything? He apparently thought I was trying to cut him out of my life. "A *famous* sister."

"No," I say, smiling at her. "It's okay. I didn't know I had a sister until a few days ago either."

"So how are you my sister if you don't live here?" she presses on. "All my friends' sisters live at their houses."

"Alison," my father says in a terse voice. "Eat your mashed potatoes."

"But Daddy!" Alison exclaims in frustration. "I'm just asking her a question!"

"It's fine," I say.

"Alison, you and Star have the same daddy," Lynda explains.

"But I've been off living with my mom," I say.

"Why?" she asks. "Why don't you just live with us?"

I push some mashed potatoes around on my plate. "Actually," I say to my father, "I was going to ask you about that."

"About what?" my father asks blankly.

"About whether I could maybe stay for a little while," I

say nervously. "Here. If you have room. You know. So I can get to know you again?"

I watch him, my heart pounding, as I wait for a reply. He and Lynda exchange glances. My father clears his throat.

"Star, I'm not sure we have enough space for you," he says. "I mean, as you can see, our house is quite small."

I glance around. It doesn't look *that* small. Then again, I suppose my perception may be skewed from living in a tiny motel room—and an even more cramped apartment — all week. But perhaps what my father is really saying is that he just doesn't want me. My heart sinks.

"I don't take up much room," I say softly. My father glances at Lynda again.

"Well," he says. "Maybe if we had a bigger place. But we're kind of pressed for money right now. With the rent at the store and all, I don't think—"

"I could help," I say instantly, before I've even thought about it. But what's there to think about? My dad needs money and I have it. Well, I *will* have it once I call my mom. My father looks surprised. "I mean, if that's the issue, I could help," I continue quickly. "Once I go back to my normal life, I'll be able to access my own accounts. I have plenty of money. I can help you buy a bigger house. I mean, it's no problem."

"That's very generous of you, Star," my father says, smiling at me warmly, "but sweetheart, I don't want you to feel like you *have* to do that."

My heart leaps to hear him call me sweetheart.

"Don't be silly," I say. "I'm your daughter. I want to help."

I feel like I'm on top of the world that night as I hug Lynda, Alison and my father good-bye and climb back into my Beetle after dinner.

Lynda murmurs something to Alison and she walks up to my car window.

"Star?" she says. "You're a cool sister."

"You're a cool sister too," I say. She shocks me by leaning forward and kissing me on the cheek. I look up at my father and Lynda in surprise. They're both smiling at us. Lynda steps forward and guides Alison away from the curb.

"See you tomorrow for lunch, honey," my father says warmly. He raises his hand and the three of them wave as I pull away from the curb.

I watch them in the rearview mirror as long as I can. Then I smile to myself the whole way back to the motel.

For the first time in my life, I feel like I might have a chance at a real family.

★

Chapter 18

*N*ick is waiting for me outside my door when I climb the stairs to the apartment above the restaurant that night.

"I'm sorry," he blurts out. "I'm really sorry about last night. I didn't know what to say. And I felt stupid for not recognizing you."

"Don't feel like that," I say with a small smile. "My own dad didn't even know me at first."

"Look, can I come in for a minute?" he asks.

In the tiny room, Nick sits down on the edge of the bed, and I sit beside him. I tell him quickly about seeing my dad today and about meeting my stepmother and half sister. I'm still in shock. Nick hugs me tightly and tells me he's happy for me.

"Star," he begins haltingly. "Or Amanda or whatever. Geez, this is weird. I don't even know what to call you."

I'm surprised to realize that his words bother me.

"I like Amanda." I give him a half smile. "I'm not exactly the biggest Star Beck fan right now. She's pretty much screwed up my life."

Nick rakes a hand through his hair. "Maybe it's none of my business. But I thought you said you weren't dating anyone."

I blink at him.

"What?" I ask. "I'm not."

"But everyone knows you're dating Jesse Bishop," he continues uncomfortably. "I mean, it's not like I follow all that gossip or anything. But I'd have to be living under a rock not to know about you and him."

Nick's trying to sound tough. But I think he looks sort of hurt.

"Oh," I say. I feel terrible. "Is that why you left so quickly last night?"

Nick shrugs.

"I just don't know why you lied to me," he says. "I mean, I understand that you're trying to blend in or whatever. But you could have told me you have a boyfriend. Especially considering that your boyfriend is, like, one of the most famous people in the country."

"Nick," I say slowly. I want to make sure he really, really hears me. "I'm not dating Jesse. I swear. I never was. It's all a stupid publicity thing. I've known him forever. He's like my brother."

Nick still looks suspicious.

"You don't have to lie to me, Amanda," he says. "I'm not going to tell anyone who you are or anything. You can trust me."

"I know I can," I say. "That's why I told you. But Nick, I'm telling you the truth about Jesse."

"But I've seen pictures of you kissing him," he protests.

"Nick, I'm an *actress*," I say. "We were acting. It was all for the publicity. It was stupid. But that's all it was. I swear."

He studies my face for a moment, and I don't let my gaze drop from his eyes. I want him to know I'm not lying. Not about this.

"Okay," he says finally. He shoots me an uncomfortable half smile. "Well, is there anything else I should know about you, while we're at it?"

"Yeah," I say. He looks concerned for a split second. "Just that I like you," I say quickly. "A lot. And I'm glad you know the truth about me."

"Yeah," Nick says after a minute. "Me too."

The next day, I meet my father for lunch at the Columbia, a nice restaurant on the Pier downtown that overlooks the water and the Tampa skyline from floor-to-ceiling windows on the fourth floor.

"The house salad's really good here," says my father as he lays the white linen napkin across his lap. "I thought you might like this place."

"It's perfect," I say with a smile. Truth be told, I could probably be dining with my father in a run-down shack in the woods and it would still feel perfect. I can't quite get over the fact that this is really happening. I'm really here, sitting across the table from the father I thought I'd lost forever, talking about something as normal as a salad.

"I'm sure you're used to restaurants that are much fancier," says my father after a moment.

"No, not really," I say.

"Oh come on," my father says, leaning forward and

winking at me. "You can tell your old man. You probably eat at all the hot spots. The Ivy. Mr. Chow's. All those places I read about in *People*. I read all the celebrity magazines to see if you're in there, you know."

"Um, no," I say with a shrug. "I really don't eat at places like that. I usually just eat backstage. Before the show."

"Well, that's nice," my father says, leaning back in his seat and nodding approvingly. "You don't brag about your lifestyle. I like that. It's classy."

I'm confused by how he's acting, but I force a pleasant smile. I'm trying to put myself in his shoes. He probably feels really out of step with my life. I feel bad for him.

"It was nice to meet Lynda and Alison last night," I say as a waiter fills our water glasses and quickly disappears.

"They enjoyed meeting you too," my father says. "In fact, Alison was talking just this morning about how much she hoped we could buy a house so we could all be a family together."

I smile. "That would be really nice," I say.

"It would be nice to have you home," he says.

We make small talk for a while, while we wait for our food, but I'm hanging on his every word, no matter how trivial.

"I just can't believe this," I say to my father after our entrees have been delivered. My salad, which the waiter tossed at the table, looks great, and my father looks pleased with his steak, plantains and rice.

"The food?" my dad asks, his mouth already full with a big bite of steak. "I know, it's great, isn't it?"

"No," I say. "Not the food. I mean, it's good. But I mean *this*. Me and you. I can't believe I'm eating lunch with my father. I thought I would never see you again."

"Yeah," my father says as he puts another forkful of steak into his mouth.

"What made you start writing to me?" I ask. It's the question I'm dying to know the answer to.

"I missed you," my father says simply. He takes another sip of water. "Because you're my little girl."

"But why didn't you write before that?" I press. "Or try to find me?"

My father looks surprised. "How do you know I didn't?" he asks.

"Did you?" I ask.

He shrugs. "Star, I never stopped loving you," he says. "You have to know that. I never stopped wondering where you were."

"So you tried to get in touch with me before you started writing me the letters every month?" I can't help it.

"Hey, I'm your old man, aren't I?" he says with a smile. "What do you think?"

"So you did?" I ask. It's like we're speaking two different languages.

"Of course, Star," he says "Hey, listen. Before I forget. I got you something."

He digs in his pants pocket for a minute and pulls out a little box.

"For me?" I ask. I look at it incredulously; then I look back up at him. "You got me a present?"

My dad shrugs.

"Can't a father spoil his little girl without it being a big deal?" he asks with a grin.

"I don't even know what to say," I begin, feeling emotional all of a sudden.

"Just open it, Star," my dad says. I nod and gently pull off the ribbon, then the wrapping paper. Inside is a little black jewelry box. I slowly crack it open and see a little silver letter *M* hanging on a silver chain.

"*M?*" I ask my dad. He smiles.

"For Mecham," he says. "Your real last name. To remind you that you're one of us again."

I can feel tears well in my eyes as he helps me put it on.

"It's beautiful, Dad," I say. I realize it's the first time I've called him that to his face since I was a kid. It feels weird. But it also feels right.

I think back to that day in Tiffany's with my mom, and

reach up and touch the necklace. "It's the nicest thing any-one's ever given me."

I have to work the dinner shift at the restaurant that night. It feels weird to still be working there now that I've found my dad. I guess I visualized this all going differently. I imagined that the moment I found him, he would wel-come me back into his life—and his home—with open arms. But, I remind myself, I wanted normal, right? And most normal teenage girls have jobs. Besides, I like the peo-ple at D'Angelo's. I like that I know how to do this now. I like that I'm not a terrible waitress. And yeah, I like that I get to see Nick pretty much every time I'm here.

I have butterflies in my stomach as I start my shift. On the way out of the Columbia, I asked my dad if he and Lynda and Alison might come in for dinner tonight. I had to tell him about my job. I guess after the big bombshell of me showing up at his store, the fact that I'm temporarily working as a waitress at a small Italian restaurant didn't make him bat an eye.

"Maybe, honey," he said. "I'll see if I can close up the store early." Thinking about him coming in, I feel like I did on Christmas Eve as a kid, full of excitement and anticipation.

So I'm in a really good mood as I run pizzas and calzones back and forth between the kitchen and the bustling dining room. It's busy for a Wednesday, and at six, the height of the dinner rush, there's even a little line outside the door. Bev and her husband Louie are thrilled.

"Business is really picking up!" Louie exclaims several times throughout the evening. He keeps muttering something about getting out of the red and into the black.

Nick arrives around eight and I tell him about my lunch with my dad and show him the necklace. I make him promise to stay until closing, just in case my dad, Lynda and Alison come in. I want him to meet them.

Around nine I'm taking a brief break in the kitchen when Nick joins me. I smile at him, thinking he's come back to keep me company or something. But then I notice that his face doesn't look open and friendly. His jaw is set, and his eyes look kind of angry.

"There's someone here to see you, *Star*," he says, lowering his voice and saying that last word a bit sourly. I look at him in surprise.

"My dad!"

"Not quite," Nick says.

Just then, the kitchen door swings wide open, and when

I look up, I'm so shocked at who's standing there that it takes it a full ten seconds to register.

"Jesse?" I squeak.

"Star!" Jesse Bishop exclaims, standing in the doorway to the kitchen in all his faded-jeans-and-rock-star-tee glory. "I've been so worried! Thank God you're okay! I've been so worried about my girl!"

Before I know what's happening, he has crossed the room in three long strides, taken me in his arms, dipped my head back and pressed his lips to mine. It's not until I straighten up in shock that I notice the wall of people behind him.

There, in the doorway to the kitchen, are at least a half-dozen photographers, snapping photos like crazy, and at least a half-dozen videographers with their lights on and their cameras rolling. And in the midst of them is Nick, standing with his arms crossed over his chest, staring right at me.

"I'm so relieved to have found you, baby!" Jesse cries out, looking not at me but at the cameras. "Everyone, look who I've found working at a pizzeria in St. Petersburg! It's Star Beck!"

I went looking for another me.
I'm lost, I'm found,
I'm broken, I'm right.
My tears are gone.
How come it's you who always
finds what I've lost?

—"LOST AND FOUND," STAR BECK
ALBUM: *SECRETS OF A STAR*

★

Chapter 19

"What on earth?" Bev demands, rushing into the kitchen. She pushes her way through the wall of photographers until she's standing face to face with Jesse and me. "What's going on here?" she demands.

"Who are you?" Jesse asks.

"I'm the owner of this restaurant," Bev says. She glances at Nick, who hasn't taken his eyes off me. "And unless you have a very good explanation for being here, I'm going to have to ask you to leave."

"I've come to rescue Star Beck," Jesse says proudly.

"Who?" Bev asks. Jesse laughs.

"Star Beck?" he says. "The most famous pop star in the world. Don't tell me you haven't heard of her."

"Of course I've heard of her," Bev snaps. "I just don't see what that has to do with my restaurant."

Jesse winks at me.

"You've had her working here for the last week," Jesse says. "Going by the name Amanda Pepper, I believe." He nods toward me. Bev turns and studies my face. Something in her expression shifts.

"Amanda? Is this true?"

I hesitate, then miserably nod. I can't believe it. Here, in front of the whole world (via the video cameras), the jig is up, so to speak. I can't believe Jesse's doing this.

Bev stares at me for a moment, then turns back to Jesse with her eyes flashing.

"Well, it doesn't look to me like she needs any rescuing right now," Bev says firmly. I feel a slight surge of pride and gratefulness. I hear one of the cameramen snicker. "As for you," Bev says, turning her attention to the media horde. "This is private property. I'm going to give you thirty seconds to get out before I call the police."

"You can't do that," one of the cameramen says.

"Watch me," she responds, her voice as cold as ice. Apparently, it's enough to convince them. After a moment of mumbling, the photographers and cameramen back reluctantly out of the kitchen, leaving the four of us—me, Jesse, Nick and Bev—alone with Max, one of the cooks, who's staring at us from the corner.

"Now," Bev says sharply, turning to Jesse. "What do you think you're doing barging in here like this?"

"Relax, lady," Jesse says innocently. "I'm just coming to get my girlfriend."

"Girlfriend?" Bev asks, turning to look at me again. I don't think it's my imagination that her face doesn't look quite as sympathetic as it did a moment ago.

I open my mouth to protest, but Jesse puts an arm around my shoulder. "Don't tell me you don't know that the press calls us pop music's prince and princess!"

Nick's eyes flash. He turns and strides quickly out of the kitchen.

"Wait! Nick!" I call after him. But he doesn't turn back. I start to go after him, but Jesse grabs my arm.

"Let him go, Star," he says softly. "The media's out there. It'll just create a scene."

My heart sinks. I stand there for a moment, looking in the direction Nick disappeared and feeling hopeless. Everything feels like it's unraveling.

"Jesse, what *are* you doing here?" I demand, finally

turning to him. "And why did you have to do that whole girlfriend thing? I really like that guy who just stormed out of here!"

I glance at Bev, who's looking at me as if I've sprouted another head. "I really like Nick," I say, turning to her. "And I swear, Jesse Bishop is *not* my boyfriend. In fact," I say, turning back to Jesse and glaring at him, "I kind of hate his guts right now."

"I see," Bev says slowly. "Well. I'll leave you two to talk."

"But Bev . . . ," I say, hating that she's about to walk away without giving me a chance to explain.

"We'll talk later," she says, shooting me a look. She turns to walk out of the kitchen. "Max!" she calls over her shoulder as she goes. Shooting me one last look, the cook drops his spatula and scampers after her too. Jesse and I are alone.

"Jesse," I say after a moment. He's standing there smiling proudly at me. But I know him well enough to be able to read the guilt in his eyes too. "What do you think you're doing?"

"Aw, Star, you don't belong here," he says. "You don't want to be *normal*." He reaches out and tries to take my hands in his, but I yank them away and glare at him. "Fine," he says. "Be that way."

"Jesse," I say. I don't even know where to begin. "I *like* being normal."

"Oh come *on*, Star," Jesse says with a laugh. "You're going to tell me you want to be a waitress instead of a pop star, and date some guy whose parents own a restaurant?"

I stiffen.

"What's so wrong with that?" I ask.

Jesse laughs.

"For God's sake, Star, what's in this pizza sauce?" he asks, gesturing to an uncooked pizza sitting out on the counter. "Crack? Did you forget who you really are?"

"Jesse," I say. "Maybe this *is* who I really am."

"Yeah. Gee, I love the glasses. And the choppy hair—nice. Interesting color too."

I glare some more and he takes a step closer. He puts a hand on my arm, and I shrug him away.

"Oh, come on, Star, I'm just kidding," he says. "This is *me*! Lighten up!"

"It's not funny, Jesse," I say coldly. He stares at me for a minute.

"Star, this is crazy!" he says finally. Now he looks concerned. "This whole thing! I just wanted to come remind you who you really are. No one knows better than me. I've known you forever!"

"Obviously, you don't know me at all," I snap.

"What are you talking about?"

"If you knew me, Jesse, you would have known that when I called you the other day, it was because I needed a friend," I say quietly. "Not because I was hoping you'd come

235

in here with a bunch of TV cameras to mess everything up. If you knew me, Jesse, you wouldn't have ruined everything."

He looks stung. "But Star," he says. "This is going to be great for our careers. This will be the lead story on the news channels for at least the next twenty-four hours. 'Pop Prince Finds Pop Princess!' It's pure gold, Star! Seriously, we'll probably each sell like twenty-five thousand records off the publicity this week alone."

I stare at him for a long time.

"You're a selfish jerk," I finally say. His eyes widen in surprise. "Nothing matters to you but album sales and publicity and your own needs," I continue. "You didn't care that you were screwing up my life." I blink back tears and head for the door. I can't even stand to be in the same room with him anymore.

"And Jesse?" I add, putting my hand on the door handle. "It's not Star. It's Amanda."

He's still staring at me as the back door swings closed behind me, leaving him standing in the kitchen alone.

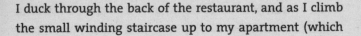

I duck through the back of the restaurant, and as I climb the small winding staircase up to my apartment (which

I'm probably no longer welcome in), I can hear Jesse speaking to the media horde in the dining room.

"Star's doing just fine," I hear him say as I reach my door. I roll my eyes. "We just need a little privacy before we talk to all of you. I haven't seen her in a week, you know."

I don't have to wait around to realize that Jesse's probably raising a suggestive eyebrow at the camera and that at home, people watching on the news will assume that Jesse and I are going to be in the restaurant making out or something equally revolting.

Jesse's prediction comes true. Finding me is the lead story on every news broadcast that night.

"Star Beck hadn't been seen since last Wednesday, a week ago today," says the solemn-looking reporter for the local NBC affiliate on the eleven o'clock news. She's standing outside D'Angelo's, talking live to the anchors, and there's a sea of media behind her. "Her mother, Laura Beck, insisted that Star was in seclusion, recuperating after her tour, and most reports had her in rehab at Lovesdale, in upstate New York. But tonight, in a strange turn of events, Jesse Bishop, Star's longtime boyfriend, found her, disguised with glasses and a short blond bob, working at D'Angelo's Ristorante on Fourth Street in St. Petersburg."

Footage of my shocked reaction in the kitchen begins to roll, and I switch rapidly to another channel.

"No one knows why Beck, a two-time Grammy winner, would run away and disguise herself . . . ," the reporter on ABC is saying. I flip again.

"Who would have thought she'd wind up in the Tampa Bay area?" the reporter on CBS is saying. I flip back to NBC and see Jesse outside the restaurant with a bank of mics stuck in his face.

"I just love her so much," he's saying. "And I'm so relieved to have found her safe and sound."

I groan and turn off the television. I flip on the radio, but of course the deejays are talking about me too, so I turn it off. Well, so much for anonymity. At least no one seems to know I'm staying at the restaurant. It's probably only a matter of time before Jesse figures that out and blabs it to the media too.

I try calling my father, but no one picks up. I leave a message asking him to call me, no matter what time it is, as soon as he gets the message.

I call Nick's cell, and he doesn't answer. So I wait another five minutes and call him again. Still no answer. It's not until I've dialed his number eleven times (okay, so perhaps I'm bordering on stalkerish here) that he finally picks up.

"Nick!" I blurt out before he can hang up. "Don't hang up."

His voice sounds weary. "Look, I really don't want to talk right now. Don't you have Jesse Bishop to make out with?"

"Come on. I'm not dating Jesse. I promise. I'm furious that he came here and did this."

"I want to believe you, but that's a little hard when you two are plastered all over the news kissing."

"I swear I'm telling you the truth," I plead.

"Like you did when you said your name was Amanda? And made yourself out to be just an average person?" Nick asks.

I blink back tears. "That was different," I say softly. "And I told you the truth about that."

Nick sighs. "I just . . . I just didn't sign up for this, you know? I wasn't even looking for a girlfriend. I certainly wasn't planning to fall for some pop star."

"You fell for me?" I ask, feeling a flutter of hope.

"Before I knew who you were," Nick says. His words hit me as hard as if he'd punched me in the gut, and I can't speak. Nick sighs. "I'm sorry. I just need to do some thinking."

"I know," I say. Then I feebly add, "Look, I'm sorry."

"I'm sorry too," Nick says, and clicks off.

I draw my knees up to my chest, hug them close and stare at the wall for a long time. Nick doesn't call back. My father never returns my message. I feel more alone than ever before.

An insistent pounding on my apartment door wakes me up at four-fifteen in the morning. I wonder how long I've been asleep as I blink several times, adjusting to the darkness, and finally struggle out of bed toward the door.

Nick, I think, feeling hope rise inside me.

I'm not prepared for the harried-looking figure I see when I open my door.

"Mom?" I say. "What are you doing here?"

I know I'm supposed to love you
And you, you're supposed
to love me.
I thought you were what I needed,
But it was all an image,
all a mirage.
There's nothing in your heart,
And you can't be in mine.

—"CAN'T LOVE YOU ANYMORE,"
STAR BECK
ALBUM: *SIMPLY STAR*

★

Chapter 20

She looks worse than I've ever seen her. Her hair is tangled, she's not wearing any makeup, and she has flip-flops on instead of her normal designer heels. Her shirt is wrinkled, and she looks like she has aged twenty years since I last saw her.

"Honey," she says. Her eyes fill with tears, and I can't help noticing, as she stands there at the top of the narrow staircase, that she looks smaller to me than she has before. Her face looks so exhausted that for a moment, I feel sorry for her. Then I remind myself that this whole mess is basically her fault.

"How did you find me?" I ask, trying to sound cold. Her face registers surprise for a moment, as if she expected me to embrace her and be thrilled to see her instead of just standing there and looking at her angrily.

"I saw the AP wires at about nine-thirty saying that Jesse had found you. I kept calling him and calling him, then I took the first flight I could get down here. He finally called me back about an hour ago and told me where you were staying. Mariska tracked down the contact information of the people who own this place, and I reached them a little while ago," Mom continues. "Bev D'Angelo let me in. She's downstairs. The press is still camped outside. They think you're in the restaurant."

I feel mortified. I don't know what to say. I stare at my mother.

"Star, honey, can I come in?" she asks after a moment. I think she's feeling uncomfortable as I stare her down. That's really not my intention, but I can't help it that I'm mad, can I?

"Whatever," I finally say, moving aside slightly so she has to squeeze past me to get into the tiny apartment.

She avoids my glance and instead surveys the room, her eyes widening.

"This is where you've been staying?" I shrug. I refuse to mention that the motel where I spent much of the last week was *far* worse.

"Yeah," I respond, like I'm challenging her to say anything about it. "So?"

"Oh honey," she says. She looks at me in anguish. "I'm so sorry I drove you to this."

"Don't be," I say. I try to keep my voice cold, although her apology has surprised me a bit. "I like it here. Better than I liked my life in your world, anyhow."

"Look," she says. "I know I haven't been the perfect mother . . ."

I roll my eyes.

"That might be the understatement of the year," I say. "Let's see: you've kept me from my father, you've lied about I don't even know how many things, and you've made me look foolish to the media. How am I doing so far?"

The more I talk, the angrier I feel. Because of her, I don't even know who I am anymore.

"Star," she says. I cross my arms over my chest and stare at her as she continues. "I am *sorry*. I just got so swept up in things, so carried away . . ." She pauses. She shakes her head. "No. It's not just that. I know I made a lot of bad decisions. But honey, you have to forgive me and realize that I'm trying to do what's best for you now."

"Yeah, because you have a real track record of honesty," I say sarcastically. Mom's face looks pained, but I don't care.

"Honey, I need to know something," she says slowly. "Have you found your father?"

"What do you care?" I snap.

"Because, Star, he's bad for you," Mom says.

I just stare at her, all the anger and stress from the last week rolling up inside me into a tight little ball.

"Oh, *he's* bad for me?" I demand. I can't seem to control the volume of my voice anymore. "I can't even believe you would say that, since you're the one who took me from him. I mean, that's basically kidnapping, isn't it?"

"Star," my mother says, her voice surprisingly calm. She looks me in the eye, and her voice sounds oddly gentle. "I didn't leave him. *He* left *us.*"

I stare at her.

"That's not what the *Dial* reporter said," I say coldly.

"I know. Mariska told me," Mom says, her voice firm. "But the reporter was wrong. Star, look at this."

She hands me a faded sheet of paper on letterhead from a law firm called Kovac, Jaye and Tan. I stare at her for a moment, then begin to read it reluctantly, feeling tears blur my vision.

It's a letter, dated thirteen years ago, apparently drafted and signed by my father, saying that he revokes all custodial rights to his child, Amanda Star Beckendale-Mecham, age three. I read the letter twice, willing myself not to cry. I look back at Mom.

"This isn't real," I whisper. "You're lying again."

"No, Star, I'm not," she says sadly. "I don't blame you for feeling that way. But honey, he walked away from us. He walked away from *you*. And yes, he's been writing to you every month, and maybe I've been wrong to keep his letters from you. But don't you understand? You hit it big six years ago, and that's when he started writing. He doesn't want to *know* you. He wants to *use* you. I've been trying to protect you from him."

"That's not true," I say, unable to stop my voice from shaking. My head suddenly hurts, and my eyes are burning. My stomach is swimming uncomfortably. "He started writing to me because he loves me. He wants to have a relationship with me. You just can't stand the thought of anyone other than you having any control over me."

Mom looks at me with an expression on her face that I know I'm supposed to interpret as sad. But honestly, I can't tell anymore what's a lie and what's not. And how am I supposed to trust her after everything she's done?

"Honey, he wants your money," she says. "Not you. I'm so sorry."

Something in me snaps.

"How dare you?" I yell at her. "How dare you say something like that? You hide his letters from me and make me think I basically don't even have a father, and then when I finally find him and have a chance at a normal life, you come in with all these lies and try to screw it up! How do you even live with yourself?"

There are tears in Mom's eyes now too, but I don't feel bad.

She looks at me for a moment and then turns away. She paces the room a few times while I stand near the door, watching her suspiciously. Then she sits down on the corner of the bed, reaches into her shoulder bag and pulls out a big manila envelope.

"Here," she says. She thrusts the bulging envelope toward me. "All the letters your father has ever written to you. Read them yourself, Star. They're almost all asking you for money."

I stare at the envelope, but I make no move to take it.

"You're lying," I say in a low voice. "It's not true. The letter the *Dial* reporter gave me just says he loves me and misses me."

I know this because I've memorized every word of it.

"She happened to get her hands on one of the few that aren't like that," Mom says softly. "But most of them are. Read them yourself."

246

I stare at the envelope for another moment. Then I turn away.

Her sad, imploring, guilty face, the letter from the law firm, the manila envelope . . . I can't take it anymore. She obviously wants to destroy any chance I have at happiness. "Get out," I say in a low, firm voice. "Get out now. I don't want to listen to any more of your lies."

"Star!" my mother exclaims. She stands up from the bed and looks at me. "Think about this. Think about what you are doing."

"Just leave, Mom," I say. "For once, listen to what I am saying."

She opens her mouth as if to say something else, but then closes it and makes her way toward the door.

"I'm sorry," she says. She places the big manila envelope full of letters on the bed. "I'll be at the Hilton downtown if you need me." Then she walks out of the room without looking back.

I shut the door behind her. Then I slide down the wall to the floor, tears flowing so fast I can barely breathe.

Being the smart pop star that he is, Jesse had no choice but to help me when I called in a favor. I don't feel an ounce of pity for him as he whines to me about fielding questions from the press outside his fancy hotel—where, supposedly, the two of us are going to hold a press conference later this morning.

"I just need a little more time," I tell him over the phone, throwing on some jeans and a tee, my ratty cap, and some makeup. "You owe me that." And he grudgingly—as I knew he would—agrees.

Avoiding the cursed manila envelope, I tiptoe out the back entrance, get in my car and drive to my dad's house.

I feel bad that I might be waking Lynda and Alison as I ring the bell. To be fair, it's seven-thirty on a Thursday. Most normal people are up, right? But if my father's up, why didn't he ever call me back last night?

"Star," he says with surprise as he opens the door. He's in a gray flannel bathrobe tied over a faded black tee and red flannel plaid pants.

"Have you seen the news?" I ask immediately.

"What?" he says. "Oh yeah. About your boyfriend coming to find you and all."

"He's not really my boyfriend," I protest, a bit mystified by his reaction. He doesn't seem at all troubled that I've been exposed.

"Well, whatever you want to call him," he says. "That famous guy, Jesse, you're always going around with.

Anyhow, yeah, so that was interesting. Good publicity for you, huh? Actually, I figured you'd be off with him somewhere today."

I stare at him. He doesn't seem to get how important this is. "Mom showed up last night, at my door," I tell him.

This, he reacts to.

"What?" he demands, his whole face suddenly coming alive. "Your mother? What did *she* want?"

"I don't know," I say, not quite sure why I'm not telling him about her accusations about him. It just doesn't feel right. Maybe I don't want to think about it. "I guess she wants me to come home with her."

"Well, honey, eventually you're going to have to go back," he says gently. I look at him in surprise.

"I thought you said I could maybe move in with you if we got a bigger house," I say.

He shrugs. "Sure, sweetheart," he says. "But you also have a career to worry about. We can't just let that fall by the wayside."

"No," I say slowly. "I guess we can't."

"Anyhow, come in." He steps aside. "Lynda's taking Alison to school. Can I make you some coffee?"

"I don't really feel like coffee right now," I reply.

Ten minutes later, we're sitting across from each other at the kitchen table, me with a glass of orange juice and a bowl of slightly stale Cheerios that I'm only pretending to eat out of politeness, and my dad with a mug of black coffee and a bagel.

"I need to ask you something," I begin after watching Dad take three huge bites out of his bagel. He chews with his mouth open.

"Okay," he says mid-bite, looking at me and waiting for me to speak. I draw a deep breath and try to sound as nonaccusatory as possible.

"Did you leave Mom?" I ask. "Or did Mom leave you?"

My father swallows his mouthful of bagel and cream cheese and takes a long sip of his coffee. My stomach is swimming, and my heart is pounding.

"What did she say?" he asks. "Did you ask her?"

"She said you left us."

My father sighs. He studies the inside of his coffee mug intently, and I suspect that he's intentionally avoiding my gaze. I remind myself to breathe properly, like my vocal coaches have taught me. I keep wanting to hold my breath.

"Star, relationships are very complicated," he begins slowly. I blink at him. This isn't exactly an answer. "Your mother and I tried to work things out. We really did. She's a wonderful lady, your mom. But sometimes you think you're compatible with someone and then things change."

"You're not answering my question."

My dad looks sideways at me and exhales loudly.

"If I could go back and change things, Star, I would," he says. "I made some mistakes that I'm not proud of. Your mom and I, we weren't right for each other. And I had to make a decision to save us both from being miserable for the rest of our lives."

"So you left her?" I ask him. "You left *us*?"

My father nods slowly. "But I wasn't leaving you, honey. This was between your mother and me. I never meant to leave you."

"But you signed away custody," I say. "Mom showed me the letter from your attorneys."

A shadow crosses my father's face.

"She did?" he asks.

I don't want to cry. I want to understand his explanation. I try my best to listen.

"I was a lot younger then," he says. He looks down at his mug for a while then back up at me. His eyes meet mine. "It was a mistake. A serious, stupid mistake that I've spent my whole life regretting."

"You've regretted it because I became famous?" I ask, trying to keep my voice from shaking. "Or because you missed seeing me grow up?"

"Oh, Star!" my father exclaims. "No, it wasn't the fame thing! I hated missing your childhood. Those are years we can never get back, and that's my fault for throwing that away. I'm so sorry."

I think about this for a minute. He sounds sincere.

"But how could you just walk out on your own child?" I ask. I'm trying hard to understand. I really am. My father pauses for a moment.

"I was a different man then," he says. "And I made a mistake that will haunt me for the rest of my life."

Dad excuses himself to clear our dishes. He leaves the room to go change out of his robe and pajamas. While he's gone, I try to get a hold of myself.

Okay, so he's not perfect, I say to myself. *But he admitted leaving and he admitted making a mistake. He's trying to make up for it now.*

I believe this. Or I nearly do. I know I *want* to. But there's a little voice in my head that says if Mom was telling the truth about him being the one to walk away from us, maybe she's right about the other things she said about him too.

I don't want to think that.

But I know I need to find out. Suddenly, I wish I had reached into that manila envelope and read a few of the letters, even if I didn't believe Mom.

I realize suddenly that if I want to find out the truth, I'm going to have to test him somehow. Otherwise I'll never know. I think about what to say to him. By the time he returns a few minutes later and settles back down across from me, I have an idea. I hate to lie, but in this case, it's for the greater good, which I figure makes it okay, just this once.

"Dad, Mom showed up because she needed to talk to me about something really important," I say.

He's listening.

"Well, it turns out our financial planner has been embezzling our money," I lie. "We thought we had millions. But he's mismanaged a lot of our finances, and he's also been gambling on the side."

I know I'm being convincing because Dad's eyes have widened in apparent horror. I press on.

"Anyhow, so Mom just found out how bad it all is," I say slowly. "It turns out that we've lost everything. And now we're, like, several million dollars in debt. It's going to take me a few years of CD sales and concerts and stuff to even get us back to where we started. And that's only *if* my album sales are good. It's pretty terrible," I add dramatically.

My father's jaw has dropped, and he's just staring at me.

"There's . . . there's no way to get the money back?" he asks finally. I'm watching him closely, and so far, I could chalk his reaction up to his being a concerned parent. "I mean, can't the police do something if this guy's been stealing your money?"

"No." I shake my head sadly. "Mom signed over all the finances to him. We don't have any legal recourse. We're in trouble, Dad."

"That stupid woman," my father says under his breath. I raise an eyebrow at him. "I should have figured she'd screw things up."

"It's not really Mom's fault," I say. He opens his mouth to say something, but I keep talking. "Anyhow, it doesn't matter whose fault it is. It matters that the money's gone. We even had to sell the tour bus."

"What?" my father asks. "What about your mansion in Los Angeles?"

I'm starting to get a bad feeling in the pit of my stomach.

"Foreclosed," I say.

"But . . . ," my father begins, then stops. He looks stricken, and there's a note of panic creeping into his voice. "But you said you could help us out with money. To buy a house. Maybe to pay the rent at the store."

My insides have started turning cold.

"I wish I could," I say flatly. I shrug again and hold my palms up helplessly. "I had no idea how bad our situation was until last night."

"There's no way of getting it back?" Dad asks, incredulous. "You're sure?"

"I'm sure."

"And it will take you years to get out of debt?"

"If we're ever able to get out." Real tears well in my eyes. "I mean, if my next CD doesn't do well, we'll have to file for bankruptcy. Even if it goes platinum, we'll probably still be in debt."

"My God," my father mutters, shaking his head.

"So I was thinking," I say, going in for the kill, hoping with all my heart that my dad will pass this test, "I was thinking that maybe I could stay with you until things get better. I mean, after a few years, I could probably give you a few thousand dollars for rent. But right now, things are tight."

He's shaking his head and talking to himself. I press on, unable to stop myself now.

"I know you said your place is small," I continue. "But I don't take up much room. I can share a room with Alison. Or sleep on the couch. I mean, the alternative is pretty much that I'm out on the street."

"Well, I don't see how that's my problem," my father says. My heart sinks. I can't believe it. He looks slightly dazed.

"It's *not* your problem," I say. "I mean, it doesn't have to be. But I'm your daughter. I'm asking for your help."

"I don't have any responsibility in this," my father says. Every word he speaks feels like it's stabbing directly into my heart. "I've terminated my parental responsibilities. Ask your mother. It's all there in the court documents. She signed them too."

"I know," I say. I feel desperate. I want so much for him to have a different reaction. "I know you don't legally have to support me. But you seemed so happy to see me. I was hoping that since you're my dad, you'd be willing to help me get on my feet. Just for a little while."

"This is ridiculous," my father mumbles to himself. He looks sharply at me. "Why wasn't this in the newspapers? Why didn't I know about this?"

I shrug, my heart heavy. It's taking every ounce of self-control not to react visibly.

"What am I supposed to do now?" my father demands, his eyes flashing.

"You?"

"Yeah, me!" he says. He seems to be getting angrier as he goes. "I mean, I put six years into finding you, writing to you, trying to get you to come find me. Finally, you do, but it's only *after* all the money's gone? Why didn't you tell me this? What, are you trying to milk me for *my* money?"

My head hurts. My eyes hurt. Everything hurts.

"No!" I say in a small voice. "I thought you wanted to be my dad again."

"Did you even read the letters?" he demands. "You *know* I need money! Are you just trying to get back at me? Huh? Is that it? Has this whole week just been an act on your part?"

"An act on *my* part?" I ask, incredulous. I don't even bother lying. "No. I just wanted to find my father again."

"Well," my father says, rolling his eyes and throwing his hands up in the air. "Are you happy now? You've found your father!"

I stare at him long and hard for a moment. It feels like there's a giant void inside me. I'm stunned, shocked, devastated. I say the only thing I can think of. "No, I didn't find my father."

My father snorts. "What are you talking about?" he asks. "I'm your father."

"No, you're not," I say sadly. "I've made a mistake. I'm pretty sure that the father I thought I remembered never existed in the first place."

★

Chapter 21

*O*kay, *breathe*, I tell myself as I pull up in the turn lane on Fourth Street. There's a swarm of at least a dozen television satellite trucks out front of D'Angelo's, clustered around the back entrance. Big men carrying big television cameras are sitting on the curb, smoking cigarettes, eating candy bars, talking to each other. Women with perfectly combed hair, tailored suits and microphones stand around in little groups, chatting and glancing toward the door. My heart sinks even further, which I didn't realize was possible. Jesse could only hold the sharks off for so long. Now I no longer have even a temporary home. I merge back into traffic before anyone notices me.

A mile up the road I pull into a strip mall. There's a pay phone outside a Starbucks.

I take a deep breath, pick up the receiver, drop in some coins and dial.

"Thank you for meeting me," I say softly when Nick sits down on the bench beside me.

Nick, who seems to hate my guts. Nick, who is upset that I'm Star Beck. Nick, who preferred me as a waitress named Amanda Pepper.

"Whatever," he says with a shrug.

"Thanks for answering on my third attempt too," I say. I give him a half smile. "I was almost out of change."

"I should have picked up sooner," he says. "I would have saved you some quarters."

We sit in silence, staring out toward Tampa Bay. Several

tall office buildings stand behind us, and the water and the distant skyline of Tampa stretch out ahead. In a way, I feel like I'm in a little bubble of safety.

"I like it here," I say finally. Joggers run by occasionally on the trail in front of us, but no one is looking at me, staring at my face, pointing and crying out that they've found the missing pop star.

"Me too," Nick says. But he doesn't offer any more.

"Nick," I begin after a moment. "I know I owe you an apology. I know you feel like I lied to you. . . ."

"You *did* lie to me," he interrupts pointedly.

"I know," I say. I sigh. "But I told you the truth as soon as I could. I *had* to lie, or it would have been just like that media circus last night from day one."

"I know," Nick says after a pause. "And I don't blame you."

I look at him in surprise.

"You don't?" I ask.

He shakes his head slowly and looks out at the bay.

"No," he says. "I did at first. I felt pretty stupid for not recognizing you. I mean, I've spent a ton of time with you in the last week. And it's not like I've never seen your picture before. But it's not that, though. I'm not mad anymore that you lied about who you are. I mean, I understand."

He pauses and looks over at me. "It's just . . . I don't know how to act around you anymore," he says. "I've never known anyone famous. And I don't know what to believe. I mean, seeing Jesse Bishop kiss you last night was really crappy for me. Obviously the whole world knows about you two being 'pop's power couple' or whatever. How do I compete with that?"

"You don't *have* to," I say.

"Sure, you say that now," Nick says. "But what happens when you two make up? Or when Prince Harry or some movie star or some guy in a boy band asks you out? Amanda, I'm just some college guy who doesn't even have enough money to move out from under his parents' roof. How do I compete with those other guys?"

I reach for his hand. "Nick, most of the guys in my world are totally fake and just looking for a headline. I don't want that."

Nick doesn't let go of my hand. I concentrate on the feeling of his fingers intertwined with mine. I feel like things are spinning out of control everywhere around me, but somehow, this feels safe. His hand is like an anchor. I hold on tighter, and after a moment, he squeezes back.

"You have your pick of probably any guy in the whole world," Nick whispers, even though no one else is around to hear him.

"Yeah," I say. I pause and wait until he looks at me. "Maybe I do. And I pick you."

Eventually, I tell Nick everything. I tell him about my mom, about her lies, about what I hoped would happen with my dad and about what happened today. I tell him about the manila envelope full of letters and about the note from my dad's attorney where he signed away all responsibility for me. But this time I don't cry. I think I've run out of tears. Or maybe I've just realized that my parents aren't worth the effort.

"This isn't how it's supposed to be," I say to Nick. "I mean, look at your parents. That's how parents are supposed to be with their kids."

"They're not always perfect," Nick says with a shrug.

"But at least you know they love you," I say. "At least even when they're mad, they're trying to do what's right for you."

"I think your mom *does* love you," he says.

"My mom loves my money," I mutter.

"Well, I'm not going to argue with that," Nick says. "But whether you see it or not, I think she loves you too. Deep down, at least. It sounds like she was trying to protect you from your dad. And I think that comes from a good place."

"She just didn't want him getting any of my money," I say.

"Maybe," Nick says. "But I think that at least part of it is that she didn't want you getting hurt. And even though her priorities are screwed up, she does care about what happens to you."

"How would you know that?" I ask.

"I don't think anyone can fake being that upset or that sorry," he says. I look at him questioningly. "In the press conference she gave this morning, I mean."

"*She* gave a press conference this morning?"

"Yeah," Nick says. He looks at me. "You didn't hear about it?" I shake my head and Nick continues. "She was crying in front of all the cameras, and she said she had screwed up. She said she loved you and that she had made a ton of mistakes with you."

"She did?" I'm incredulous. I can't imagine my mother admitting she's wrong about anything. Especially in public. Nick looks at his watch and stands up, pulling me with him.

"Yeah," he says. "And I bet we can catch it on the news at noon if we hurry. It starts in fifteen minutes."

We jog into a burger joint near the park at 11:58, and Nick orders two Cokes and asks the bartender to change the TV to channel eight, the local NBC station.

"Star Beck's mother apologized to her daughter in a tearful press conference this morning," the female anchor says after the newscast starts. Nick asks the bartender to turn the TV up a bit. He does so and glances at the TV, which is showing a picture of me while a reporter in the field recaps the fact that I was found last night in St. Petersburg and that I've disguised myself with short blond hair, a Dodgers cap and glasses.

The bartender looks back at me. I'm not wearing the glasses, but still, he does a double take. "Hey, you aren't Star Beck, are you?"

I nod.

"Holy crap," he says, his eyes widening. "Dude. Can I have your autograph? No one will believe me."

I nod and distractedly scribble my name on a cocktail napkin while on-screen, the reporter finally calls up video from the press conference this morning.

My mom is standing outside the Hilton a few blocks from here, wearing the same rumpled clothes she was in last night when she materialized at my door.

"It's all my fault," she says, tears flowing down her face. I stare in disbelief. I've *never* seen her cry. "I've tried to be a good mother, but I haven't always been. I've been selfish and mean, and I haven't let Star be herself. I've tried to control her."

"Oh my God," I murmur to Nick. He slips an arm around

my waist and pulls me closer. On the TV, my mom continues.

"I haven't focused enough on being a good mother," she says tearfully. "It's not her fault that she ran away; I drove her to it. I just hope she forgives me and gives me another chance."

The reporter comes back on to say that there's no word yet where I've gone but that they'll keep their viewers updated with any breaking news. Then the anchor starts talking about a two-alarm fire in a neighborhood in west Tampa.

"She looked like she really meant it," I say, feeling confused. Nick nods.

"I know," he says.

"But this doesn't change anything, does it?" I ask. "I mean, she's still been awful. And even if she *does* have some feelings about me, that doesn't change the fact that she's never been motivated by love. She's been motivated by money and fame and all the places my career can take her."

Nick nods again.

"That might be true," he says, and I know he's waiting for me to put the pieces together on my own.

"Why can't I just have normal parents?" I ask wearily.

"You know, *no* one's parents are normal," he says. I raise an eyebrow at him.

"What about yours?" I ask. I don't think I've seen anyone more normal than Bev and Louie. Nick laughs and shakes his head.

"Sure, my parents *look* normal," he says. "But they're as weird as anyone else's. They separated when I was twelve and just got back together a couple of years ago. They used to fight all the time. My dad went through this phase where he tried to grow his hair out and bought himself a red convertible. He looked ridiculous."

"What?" I laugh. Nick shakes his head.

"I know, crazy, right?" he continues. "And my mom? Yeah, when my dad moved out, she freaked and bought, like, every self-help book in the bookstore. She was always burning incense and stuff and saying things to me like, 'You need to own your feelings,' or 'Embrace your sadness,' whatever that meant. The whole time I was in high school, even when my dad moved back in, I felt like I was living in an insane asylum."

I laugh some more. "Really?" I say.

"It's all relative," Nick says with a shrug. "And who knows what goes on behind closed doors, you know? Haven't you ever wondered why my dad's barely ever at the restaurant? They only get along if they stay away from each other."

"Hmm," I say after a minute. "But at least they never stopped loving you."

"That's true," Nick says. "But you know, sometimes life doesn't work out the way you think it's supposed to."

"What do you mean?" I ask.

"Sometimes you have to play with the cards life deals you." He pauses and laughs. "I think that's one of my mom's lines from her self-help phase."

"Uh-oh, you're turning into your mom," I tease. He nudges me.

"Seriously, though," he says. "Okay, so maybe your dad is a selfish jerk and maybe your mom thinks about herself more than she thinks about you. But that doesn't mean you have to walk away from everything. It just means you have to see things for what they are. You have to realize that there are literally millions of people out there who totally adore you."

"That doesn't make up for parents who don't love me," I say softly.

"No, it doesn't," Nick agrees. "But this is your life. And you can choose to let it get you down. Or you can choose to look at all the good things, all the cool opportunities you have and all the people who really like you, and maybe think about starting over again. Don't let your mom control you. But maybe you can give her another chance to be a part of your life."

Sure, there's a lot that I *don't* like about my old life.

There's so much that's fake; there are so many stupid rules; I feel like I can never just be me. But Nick's right. Maybe it doesn't *have* to be that way. Maybe instead of walking away from it all, I can just work with what I already have and change it to make me happier.

And I'm not sure my mother deserves another chance. But if I don't give her one, maybe I'm not being any better than her.

"Can I borrow your phone?" I ask Nick. He smiles and pulls his cell out of his pocket. I punch in my mother's number.

"Mom?" I say when she answers. "I think I'm ready to come home now."

Once I ran away,
away from who I was,
Now I'm coming back
to face up to me.
I lived in lies, in my own
disguise,
But in the end, the truth
will set me free.
When you wish, when you wish,
Dreams really do come true.

—"WHEN YOU WISH," STAR BECK
ALBUM: *WHEN YOU WISH*

Epilogue

*S*even Months Later...
"Star!"
"Over here, Star!"
"I have a question!"
"Star!"
"Star!"
"Star!"

The reporters clamor for my attention, waving their arms wildly in the air. I just watch them for a minute, smiling. I'm sitting in a fancy ballroom in New York, talking to a hundred journalists about *When You Wish*, the new album we started recording the first week of December. It's my proudest accomplishment yet.

A lot has changed. The first thing I did when I got back from Florida was to hire a lawyer to help me officially take control of my finances. I fired Mariska and hired a new publicist (because after all, what kind of publicist lets me get involved in a fiasco like the one she and Jesse created—and then tells everyone I'm in rehab?). I decided that three of the songs *I* had written would go on my new album. I took Mom off the payroll as a manager (after finding out that she had set it up so that she was drawing a $750,000-a-year salary!) and added her on as a consultant at $100,000 a year. With her tail between her legs, she said yes. I told her afterward that I wouldn't need my consultant to travel with me on tour but that she was welcome to come *visit* anytime she wanted to.

In other words, I took back my life. And I'm taking back my music too.

I knew I was taking a risk with the new album, because I made it more *me*. It's less pop and more rock. The lyrics are not bubble-gum sweet; I tried to infuse them with as much honesty as I could. It's not overproduced to the point you can barely tell it's me, like my earlier stuff. And oh yeah, it's full of guitar solos from the great Ben Hudson, who's become a better friend than ever. He even produced four of the tracks on the album.

And guess what? Everyone loves it. The reviews so far have been really great. The first single, "All of Me," just hit number one on the charts this week. The best part of that is that "All of Me" is one of the songs on the album that I wrote.

I spend thirty minutes answering press questions. Yes, I'm happy to be back. Yes, I'm looking forward to the tour this summer. Yes, I'm slowly getting my relationship with my mom back on track. Yes, I'm thrilled that "All of Me" has already hit number one. No, I haven't talked to Jesse Bishop since the fall. Yes, this album is my favorite one I've done so far. Blah, blah, blah, blah.

The press conference seems to be winding down when my new publicist, Sarah, calls on a journalist in the back of the room who's been waving his hand wildly in the air.

He stands up, and I suck in a quick breath as I recognize him.

"Star," he says slowly. I stare at him, and all the reporters in the room seem to fall away. "I'm sorry I had to come to the press conference like this, but you won't take my calls. I just wanted to say I love you. We miss you. I hope you'll come home."

He looks older than last time I saw him. His hair seems

to be graying more. His green button-up shirt looks rumpled, and his posture is a little stooped. I stare at him, and all around the room, I can hear the reporters' voices buzzing.

"Is that him?"

"Is that really Star's dad?"

"Who is that guy?"

He speaks again and the reporters simmer down to listen.

"Honey?" he asks loudly. "Star, it's me. Your *dad*."

I pause and look at him for what feels like an eternity. "I'm sorry, but I haven't seen the dad I remember in thirteen years."

I half expect that when I say it, something inside me will hurt. But instead, I feel a surge of power.

"Do you want me to call security?" Sarah asks, loudly enough that the journalists can hear her.

"I don't think that's necessary," I say into my microphone, staring straight at my father. His face has contorted into an ugly sneer. "I think he can find his own way out."

With everyone staring at him, he finally stands up and walks out of the ballroom. I watch him go; then I turn to Sarah.

"I'm done," I whisper.

She nods and thanks the journalists for coming. I say good-bye, wave politely and make my way out the back door, escorted by three bodyguards. They take me back up to my suite. I insert the key card and slip inside.

"Hey, babe," says a male voice from the other room of the suite. "How did it go?"

Nick rounds the corner, looking better than ever in a Devil Rays tee, faded jeans and slightly damp hair. He's spending the summer on tour with me before he goes back to school in August.

Nick pulls me into his arms, and for a moment, I just hold on tightly, breathing him in. He smells like fresh soap and toothpaste and boy.

He tilts my chin up and touches his lips softly to mine.

"You okay?" he asks.

I smile up at him and pull him closer. He responds, hugging me back, and I burrow my face into his firm chest, feeling like I'm finally home, feeling like maybe family doesn't just have to include the people you're actually related to. Maybe the people who we love and who love us— the people who see us for who we really are—can be family too.

"Yeah," I say softly. I close my eyes and take a deep breath. "I'm better than ever."

Kristin Harmel grew up wanting to be a famous rock star, until she realized she can't sing. As in, she scares people away. So she turned to writing. *When You Wish* is her first novel for teens; she's also the author of three novels for adults: *How to Sleep with a Movie Star, The Blonde Theory,* and *The Art of French Kissing*. Kristin is a reporter for *People* magazine and appears once a month as the "Lit Chick" on the nationally syndicated morning TV show *The Daily Buzz*. She lives in Orlando, Florida, where you might catch her singing bad karaoke.